DANCING *with* DIANA

DANCING *with* DIANA

JO SALAS

CODHILL Codhill Press
New Paltz, New York

Codhill books are published by David Appelbaum for Codhill Press

First published by Tusitala Publishing 2014

Chapter Six was published as "Waiting at the Ritz" in *A Slant of Light: Contemporary Women Writers of the Hudson Valley,* Eds Carr and Zlotnik Schmidt, Codhill Press, 2013.

This is a work of fiction. Characters, names, events, and locations are either imaginary or used fictitiously.

Cover design by Tilman Reitzle/Oxygen Design

Library of Congress Cataloging-in-Publication Data

Salas, Jo, 1949–
Dancing with
Diana / Jo Salas.
pages cm
ISBN 1-930337-84-1 (alk. paper)
1.
Women—Fiction. I. Title.

PR9639.4.S25D36 2015
823'.92—dc23

2015009475

For Laurie

CHAPTER ONE

Alex

Going to boarding school was like spinning into outer space, into utter darkness and cold. I'd hardly ever been outside Westerford, let alone a hundred and fifty miles into the dreary countryside with one sodden green field after another, cows lying down, overgrown hedgerows. It didn't help that it was completely my choice to go. My father was driving, my mother beside him in the front seat. The neighbors were looking after Gillian. She was too little to understand what was happening but I had cried when I said goodbye to her and Gillian held tight to me, weeping too.

In the car we were all silent. I stared out of the rain-smeared windows and tried to summon a shred of courage. But I couldn't even locate my anger, the rage that had made me insist on finding a new school. My legs felt cramped and useless inside my new school uniform trousers. My arms wandered like underwater creatures. What on earth made me think I could cope with being away from my home, my family, my town, everything I'd ever known?

"Next turn on the left," said my mother quietly. She was reading the directions from the letter in her lap. I peered into the green gloom and saw a huge open gate, very fancy, and a long gravel driveway with oak trees on each side. I felt sick.

"Cor blimey," said my father in a sarcastic voice. Ahead of us was a grand house like one of those stately homes where tourists wallow in a fantasy of riches and aristocracy, as my dad would say. Some of those houses even had a lord and lady still in residence. You wouldn't catch my father visiting a stately home, nor my mother.

We pulled up in front of a massive front door. Beside the steps was a ramp.

They got me into my wheelchair and in we went. My first glimpse of my home for the next four years. Inside it didn't look so grand. They'd fixed everything up so that boys in wheelchairs or using crutches could get around. No carpets. Not many doors. A sign pointing to a lift to the upstairs. The furniture was faded and scuffed.

I went into a bit of a daze. Grown ups appeared and shook my parents' hands, and mine. A middle-aged woman in a nurse's uniform took us up in the lift to the dormitory where I was to sleep. Four beds. I didn't like the idea of sharing a bedroom, let alone with three other boys. Of course I'd known that this is what you did at boarding school, but it was different, actually seeing those beds. My mother had brought my red quilt and she laid it over my new bed. She stowed my stuff away in the dresser drawers. On top of the dresser she put a photo of the four of us at Saunton Sands with the sea behind us. She held up the one of Michele but I shook my head and she put it in a drawer.

My father and I watched her as though mesmerized. We were all very quiet. Shocked, I think, now that we were actually here.

The matron waited in the doorway. "Come and meet the other boys," she said. We followed her back down to the ground floor and along a wide hallway. "The common room," she said, gesturing to an open doorway. This was the biggest shock of all. I saw a big wood-paneled room full of boys who looked like me, more or less. Some looked worse, some looked better, but they were all cripples, spastics, handicapped, whatever you want to call them. Callipers, crutches, walkers, wheelchairs all over the place. It was like looking in a fun-house mirror, seeing yourself multiplied and distorted. That was how it seemed to me in that moment, anyway. When I got to know them they all seemed quite different from each other and from me.

Some of the boys looked up and nodded hello, then went on with their board games or books or watching the TV. I gave a small wave back to the ones who'd looked at me. I didn't try to say anything, since they probably wouldn't have understood. That was a big task ahead of me, getting everyone used to my weird speech.

It occurred to me that I'd have to get used to theirs.

I said goodbye to my parents at the front door. My mother and I were both trying not to cry. We'd been together every single day for fourteen years. They'd never wanted to send me away, even when everyone else thought they should. I made a massive effort to summon a smile. "I'll write to you soon," I said, trying to sound confident. My mother kissed me once more and they were gone.

There were a hundred of us at Nails. We were all in the same boat, all of us deviants from the norm, all of us weird, in need of help. And now cut off from the normal world our families lived in. I didn't find it easy to get used to this new reality. I missed my family dreadfully. And Michele. On the other hand, it was an enormous relief to be with others like me. We had our own little universe, we did things our way. There were no Adams. No one had to feel self-conscious or odd, because we all had handicaps. Crippled was normal. We were all OK in our minds, just slow in our talking and our writing, and hampered by bodies that didn't work the way they were supposed to.

I settled in, bit by bit. After a while I felt a kind of freedom that I hadn't had before. Not that I wanted to live like that forever, separated from ordinary people. But for now it was all right.

"Get a good night's sleep," said Tony one evening, a year or so after I'd come to Nails. I was fifteen by then. We were heading for bed after the usual listless hour in front of the telly in the common room, everyone sprawled around trying to enjoy themselves but feeling too tired for fun. Lugging our bodies around, on crutches or in wheelchairs, was exhausting. Tony had been one of my roommates since I'd arrived. He wasn't Michele, but we'd become friends, more or less, starting when we realized we were both Monty Python connoisseurs. We couldn't do the voices or the silly walks but I could make him remember a skit with the tiniest bit of a gesture or a face and he'd fall about laughing. It made me feel witty. Tony was in a wheelchair too. We understood each other's speech pretty well.

"Why?" I said. I meant about the good night's sleep.

Tony grinned. Spit pooled at the corner of his mouth and spilled down his chin. He dabbed at it awkwardly. "The hoity-toity girls are coming tomorrow."

I didn't know what he was talking about. But the next day, after lunch, they lined us up in the corridor and dried our faces and sponged the worst of the food stains off our striped school ties and made sure our shoelaces weren't dangling. Then they brought us all back to the dining hall. It was all cleaned up, with vases of flowers on the tables.

"Visitors!" said Miss Kimble. "You boys are very lucky. Do behave yourselves, now."

The door opened and the headmaster came in with a group of girls. Normals, not cripples. About twenty of them. They were wearing school uniforms but they looked like movie stars to me. Half of them were blond. Healthy as could be.

"What the hell?" I whispered to Tony.

He leaned over to me as best he could. "They're from Shelby." I waited for more information. "Fancy-arse girls' school, in the next village."

I was still in the dark. "Well, what are they doing here?"

Tony snickered. "They're supposed to learn how to rub shoulders with the less fortunate. That's us."

"Welcome to Tuffnall's Home for Handicapped Boys," announced Mr. Donahue. I shrank in my wheelchair. It was like being on the High Street with my mum again, bracing myself for the stares, the insults. Wishing I could hide but being stuck out in view like a headless carcass in the butcher shop.

Miss Kimble brought two of the girls over to me and Tony. She introduced us, her voice fluorescently bright. "Tony and Alex. May I introduce Annabel and Sarah."

"How do you do?" said one of them. Her voice was like the Queen saying her Christmas message, which my family found very entertaining. "Mah husband and Ah…" my mother would mimic. The girl started to offer her hand then withdrew it, her glance skittering off our curled-in paws. "This is my first time visiting your school. It's awfully nice of you to have us." She looked beseechingly at Miss Kimble, who'd stepped back a bit.

I felt sorry for the girl. For all she knew we were total morons who couldn't understand a thing she was saying. Unfortunately, I couldn't help her. She wouldn't get what I was saying. I tried to smile, with my disobedient mouth.

"Um..." she tried again. "I say, do you have riding and things like that at your school? We ride almost every afternoon, don't we, Sarah? Some of us keep our ponies on the grounds." Her cheeks were crimson. She knew she was talking rubbish. She shot a desperate look at her friend, who was as mute as me and Tony. "I say... awfully nice to meet you both." She grasped her friend's arm firmly and walked away. Tony and I chuckled as though we felt superior and relaxed. Inside I felt like crap, in a way that hardly ever happened any more. Like dried-up dog turd. Why did they let these girls come here? We were much better off by ourselves.

"Let's have some music!" cried Miss Kimble. She didn't wait for encouragement but turned and fumbled with the record player. I wasn't sure if this would make things worse or better. Worse, probably. We would just have to endure this jollity until the girls had rubbed enough shoulders, and then they would leave and we would go back to being our abnormal selves. The music piped up—a corny rock and roll song. Miss Kimble no doubt was proud of herself for choosing something on the pop charts instead of Frank Sinatra. One of the girls must have been especially bold or brave, because she grabbed the hands of a boy who looked a bit closer to normal than the rest of us. She coaxed him into an awkward dance, the two of them shuffling from foot to foot, grinning like idiots. "Come on, Philippa!" she called to her friend. Philippa looked around and pulled another boy out onto the floor. It was Robert from the sixth form, his face bright red under his freckles.

"Cripes," muttered Tony. "Don't come near me, that's all I ask." In our wheelchairs we were safe. We weren't going to be asked to dance. We stared at the handful of gorgeous girls and defective boys and their semblance of dancing. I burned for our schoolmates, made such fools of.

The music changed to a Stevie Wonder song. A girl I hadn't noticed appeared in front of me with her hands outstretched. She was tall, very blue eyes, very good-looking. She looked at me but didn't seem embarrassed the way Annabel had been. "May I?" she said. I must have nodded, or at least refrained from making a "fuck off!" gesture, because next thing I knew she had grabbed the arms of my wheelchair and wheeled me out onto the floor. She moved backwards across the room, holding my eyes, smiling but not making fun, somehow I knew for sure she was not making fun. She was dancing. I was dancing too, in my wheelchair. She made it swoop and spin in time to the music. I cried out, I couldn't help it. I put my hands on top of hers and held her wrists. They felt narrow and strong. I had never held a girl's hands, except for Michele's. Other people slid by in a blur of color. The girl was wearing some kind of flowery scent and it wafted past my nose. I could feel my face grow hot but it was excitement, not shame. The girl laughed with the pleasure of the backwards movement and it made me laugh too. I knew it was a creepy sound, my laugh, but she seemed to know it was a laugh anyway. We went around and around, up and down, until the song ended. I wished it would go on longer.

The girl wheeled me back to Tony. When we got there she ducked her head in sort of a bow. "Thank you very much." She was a little out of breath. She turned to leave and Tony called out, just clearly enough for her to understand: "What's your name, miss?"

"Dahna," she said. Di-anna, we would have pronounced it, not being posh like her. *Dah*-ana. "What's yours?"

"I'm Tony," he said, making a huge effort to make the words to come out in something like their proper shape. "This is Alex." He pointed to me.

"Thank you," I managed, knowing miserably that to her it sounded like "Anh oo." I didn't want to spoil everything by trying to talk, after our dance.

The feeling of the dance stayed in my body, the next day, the next week, the week after that. For months. It reminded me of when I watched Michele riding a horse, suddenly not handicapped at all. The feeling of swooping and gliding around the floor while Stevie Wonder wailed, the girl's blue eyes locked on mine, both of us laughing together. Being chosen by her. Me, Alex. She was a beautiful girl. It was the most beautiful moment I'd ever had in my life. The more I thought about it the more beautiful it was.

I didn't speak about it to anyone. There was no one I could talk to. Michele was the only conceivable person and she was dead. My dance with Diana, I would say to myself. I liked to say her name the way she said it, Dah-ana, but silently. The memory was like a jewel that I took out of its box and looked at every now and then, holding it up to the light to see its beauty. No one knew about my treasure.

The next year they told us that the Shelby girls were coming again. I became ill with anticipation. I had no idea if Diana would come or not. I didn't even know if she was still at the school. Maybe she'd left. I had thought she was older than me. But we were almost the same age, born in 1961, me in January, her in July. I learned that a few years later, when I and the whole world knew everything about Diana.

I imagined seeing her again, fantasizing so vividly that I exhausted myself. I imagined her recognizing me, greeting me, dancing with me again. I practiced saying her name aloud. As the day approached I worked myself up into a state of absolute dread, equally afraid that she would not come, and that she would. What if she came and didn't remember me, and didn't dance with me again? I thought I might die if that happened.

I never found out if she came or not, because when the day finally arrived I was in the infirmary. I had three seizures during the night and I was in no state to sit upright in my wheelchair, let alone dance like a fool around the flower-decorated dining room.

I tried to ask Tony without letting him know how much it meant to me. He screwed up his face trying to remember. "Oh yeah. That tall girl that took you off dancing." I waited for him to go on. "I didn't recognize her this time. Can't be sure either way."

CHAPTER TWO

August 30, 1997, morning.

She awakens with a dream in her mind. In the dream she is flying low over seawater, held in someone's arms, like a first-time skydiver in the arms of her instructor. She flies blissfully through currents of warm air. The arms holding her are a skeleton's arms. She is not afraid or repulsed. The skeleton cradles her in its bony embrace. Her head is nestled into its fleshless shoulder, its skull bent to shelter hers. Her knees are drawn up like a small child's. The sea glitters below them. They are flying across the Channel to England. Home. She wakes before they get there and feels bereft.

The Mediterranean sun is gentle, its burning heat yet to come. She wraps herself in a white robe and sits on the terrace. Thick bougainvillea shields her from the curious eyes that no doubt are already trying to find her. She does not touch the breakfast waiting under silver covers. Inside, her lover snores lightly, his arm thrown over the sheet. It is not love that they share. Transient comfort and amusement, perhaps. Physical pleasure. They hardly know each other. She picks up the filigreed coffee pot and pours half a cup. Tomorrow her August exile is over and she can go home. The dream rises in her mind again, being borne across the water in a skeleton's bony embrace. Home across the Channel. Home to her boys. She'll say goodbye to the man in her bed. He'll be disappointed, briefly. He's played his part, he and his father both, offering her a haven for this empty month. She is grateful. But now it is over.

She feels exhausted and thinks of sleeping again. She longs to sleep and wake up tomorrow, when she can go home.

She dresses and goes to sit by the bright turquoise pool, sheltered by high walls with guards outside. She stares at the slow-rippling water. There is no wind. Something must be making it move, she thinks, some hidden gadget. For my entertainment. The sequestered tranquility does not soothe her. She remembers the graveyard in Bosnia, only a few weeks ago, with the landmine people. The woman tending a grave. "Moj sin," she said, her fingertips on her heart. "My son," the translator murmured. She touched the woman's face, streaked with tears and dirt. They reached toward each other. She felt the woman sob. Comfort flowed between them.

On the plane she looks down at the wrinkled Mediterranean until the coastline of France appears, then the countryside punctuated with villages and roads and rivers far below. Her lover is playing cards and drinking with the bodyguards. The plane is furnished like a living room, white leather armchairs, a gleaming liquor cabinet, a deep-piled carpet: his father's taste. She kicks off her sandals and looks at her bare feet, manicured and tanned. She used to want to hide her feet because they were so long and clumsy. "You'll never be a princess with hoofs like those," her two older sisters teased. They all wanted to be princesses. How old was she then? Thirteen? Fourteen? It was only a couple of years later that she was singled out and thrown, an unfinished vessel, into the red-hot kiln of her engagement and marriage. I was not formed yet, she thinks. I shattered too easily. And had to glue myself together again, over and over.

A crew member hands her a glass of white wine and she takes it, smiling at the woman, warmth rising easily to her eyes.

No one was told they were coming, he swears, but when their plane lands at Orly in the afternoon the photographers are already there, as though they, with predators' acuity, could smell them approaching through the sky. His father has supplied a driver and a long black car and the photographers swarm around it like vermin. She loathes them. And yet runs her fingers through her hair and lets them see her face, this side, then that side. She can't stop herself.

They bang on the car windows, shouting her name. The black car slides away from the curb and speeds along the highway towards Paris, followed by another black car with their bags, the necessities of a month of travel. The photographers are close behind.

"Damn them!" she cries. "Make them leave us alone!"

He leans forward to the driver. "Abdel--not my apartment. The Bois de Boulogne. And lose the hyenas." The driver understands. He's brought his employer's son to this house before, accompanied by lovely women. He swerves off the boulevard just as the light turns red, the luggage-carrying SUV on its heels. A torrent of traffic blocks the road and the hyenas cannot follow.

"Bravo," she says to Abdel. "Merci." In the rear view mirror his eyes crease with pleasure.

Her lover runs around to open the car door for her and leads her through the gate of a pretty villa set back behind a thicket of trees. He throws open the front door with a flourish and shows her in. “My darling, you'll never guess who used to live here!” She looks around at the china dogs in the entranceway, the elaborate ceiling. He leads her into the drawing room. She notes the pretentious pale blue paneling on the walls.

“Guess!”

But she is studying the personal photos clustered on end tables and mantelpieces. Relics. She recognizes those arrogant faces. She's heard of this house, their last refuge in exile.

She turns around. “Do you realize who they were?”

“Yes, darling, a royal couple, from England like you. They lived here years ago.” History is a fog to him. “And it's been kept exactly as they left it! We could live here, you know. My father said we could. We could redecorate if you like.”

She stares at him. She has no intention of living with him anywhere. Least of all in this monument to shame, tainted by that vain, foolish, outcast couple.

“Well,” she says, attempting to lighten her words, “I suppose some would say this is where I belong. Since I'm the next catastrophe.” He looks uncomprehending. He does not see how that fifty-year-old scandal foreshadows hers. “I'd like to leave, if you don't mind,” she says to him, keeping her tone even.

He looks at her, disappointed, but does not argue. “Certainly, sweetheart. We'll go to the hotel, then.”

I just have to get through this day, she reminds herself. The rest of this day, and tonight, and then I go home.

The black cars wait in front, engines running.

CHAPTER THREE

Alex

The first shock was finding out that I was going to go to school after all. I was ten years old and my life was satisfactory as far as I was concerned. I spent a lot of each day doing the things I most wanted to do, with my mother's considerable help. She'd been teaching me at home ever since they'd all worked out, finally, that I was not a moron in spite of being unable to speak or control my body. The local education authority wanted to send me away to a special school but my mother refused. She knew what those places were like. I think my father would have said yes, if it were up to him. Having a son like me was tough. "Not what I signed up for," I heard him say to her once.

One day my mother came and sat beside me on the sofa. "Alex," she said, picking up my book and closing it gently, "you've been doing so well with your reading, and with your walking and speaking too. Daddy and I are very proud of you." There was something in her tone that made me wary rather than pleased, the way our cat would get tense when he knew that you were stroking him because you had to put flea powder on him, not because you loved him.

Then came the flea powder. "So we've decided that it's time for you to go to school." I stared at her. She looked so pleased. "You know Eastcott Primary School?" Of course I knew it. It was five minutes from our house, on the way to the shops. I liked seeing the kids running around the playground, though I was always a little scared they'd see me watching and shout something at me. "Well, they have a new headmistress now. She's quite young. A decent sort. We've been talking to her, us and some other parents. And she agrees with us that handicapped children should be able to go to ordinary schools."

She waited for me to chime in with a pleased comment but I was still bracing myself for the rest of it. She went on. "So she's worked very hard to arrange a special room and a special teacher, and you're going to start next week, Alex! Isn't that wonderful?"

I could talk so much better than I used to but it still took me a long time to get anything out. I was trying to say, but Mum, I like learning with you here at home, I don't want to go to school. I immediately thought of objections—how would my wheelchair fit through the doors? How would I go to the lavatory? I could manage that by myself now but it took me a very long time and my mum was there to help if I needed her. How would the teacher understand me? And the other kids?

"We've worked it out with Miss Hetherington," she said as though she'd heard me. "I'll push you there in your wheelchair, and then you'll use your crutches inside." I'd got pretty good at walking around the house, even clambering up the stairs, but I couldn't walk far. "You can use your wheels outside in the playground, if you want to. Alex, you're such a bright boy. You deserve to be in a real school. We're so pleased about this!"

I had a funny feeling that she was trying to convince herself as well as me. She'd often said she liked being my teacher, though it wasn't exactly what she'd hoped for herself. She told me all about it when I was old enough—how she got pregnant in her final year at university, and got married to my dad, and then was suddenly a very young mother of a handicapped child with no hope of finishing her degree or becoming a lawyer or a doctor as she'd expected. Taking me on as a pupil was at least a way to use her brain, she said. So why was she giving it up?

It seemed to be all decided. When I tried to argue about it my father got annoyed and said, "Do you think your mother's going to do nothing but look after you for the rest of her life?" It scared me, the idea that she might not like looking after me. I stopped arguing after that.

I had a week to get used to the idea that I'd be going to Eastcott, with ordinary kids. It was terrifying. All my life I'd had to hear horrible things from people I didn't know. When I was little, limp and awkward in my outgrown pushchair, adults would say things to my mother like "Put him in a home, dear. It's the kindest thing to do." My mother hoped, at those moments, that I was mentally disabled after all, so that I wouldn't understand what they were saying. I didn't know how to tell her that I understood everything.

The kids were worse, especially the big ones. "Cripple!" "Mental!" "Should've aborted ya!"—things like that, they said, the meanest of them. I learned then to withdraw into a place that was distant from my body. I felt safe there, unreachable. It was better if they thought I was an idiot.

Sometimes, sitting in our front window, I watched children walking to school. They swung their satchels at each other. They shared sweets or snatched them out of each other's hands and dared each other to race to the corner. Girls skipped along hand in hand. Even if they were nice to me, I couldn't see imagine being one of them. And schoolwork—it was one thing to sit with my mother, all her attention focused on me, and read books that I'd chosen from the ones she offered. But in school, even in a special room, there'd be other kids. I'd have to do the work that everyone else was doing.

I did not feel ready, not at all.

At the same time I was aware of little runnels of curiosity, even excitement. I had one friend whose mother was a teacher at the high school with my dad. Justin sometimes talked to me about his school. He liked it. He pretended to complain about homework but I could tell he didn't really mind. Sometimes he'd bring it with him when he and his parents came to visit, and we'd work on it together. From Justin and from books and kids' programs on television I knew all about spelling tests and blackboards, painting on an easel, playing on the playground, having friends.

The idea that I, weird as I was, could possibly be part of all of that was, in spite of everything, a shiny idea for me.

I didn't have a choice, anyway. My mum and dad took me along to the school one day after the other children had gone home. Miss Hetheringon and the teacher, Mrs. Avery, sat down with me and explained exactly how it would work. They tried to make it sound easy and fun. My parents got me a school uniform—grey short trousers and a grey jersey with a blue stripe around the neck, and a little blue and grey cap. I thought it was ridiculous to make me wear all this but for someone like me, everything's ridiculous. My skinny legs stuck out of the shorts. The grey socks sagged around my ankles. What I did like was my new satchel, brown leather with a brass buckle. I loved its smell. I could put my books in it, and my lunch.

On the first day my mother took me to the school after the normal kids had arrived. We left the wheelchair by the door and I lurched along the corridors on my sticks, glancing in at the classrooms packed with children in their grey and blue, reciting multiplication tables or writing at their desks. I hoped they wouldn't look up and see me. Mrs. Avery's classroom was small, much smaller than the regular classrooms, hardly bigger than our living room. It had tall windows and yellow-painted walls. Mrs. Avery said hello to me and my mother. The other children were there already, with their mothers and one of the fathers.

"A new chapter begins," said the father. He seemed very pleased but underneath I was pretty sure that he felt nervous too. "Congratulations to us all. And best of luck to you brave children!" he added, smiling at us. Brave! I felt like our cat trying to hide from the vacuum cleaner.

There were only four of us. One boy was blind, with one eye that was just white, the other wandering from side to side. There was a girl with mousy-brown plaits and callipers on her legs, and the same kind of boots that I wore. She had thick glasses and one arm was thinner than the other. I found out later that she had cerebral palsy too, though different from me and not as bad. I had the floppy kind, while she had the scrunched-up kind. She could talk normally, and she didn't have to use a wheelchair at all. The third was a Mongoloid boy, short and roly-poly, his face split by a constant smile. Down's syndrome, we'd say now. Clive didn't seem nervous like the rest of us. I learned later that the girl, Michele, had gone to a small village school before coming to Eastcott. The two boys had been in boarding schools. Their families were very happy that now they could live at home again.

Our parents said goodbye to us. Roger, the blind boy, was sniffling. His father patted his arm firmly and told him to be a good boy. I could easily have cried too but I didn't want my mother to worry. And, along with being scared, I was excited.

Somewhere in me I knew that it actually didn't matter so much how I felt or what my mother and father wanted. Here I was, out in the world, sort of, with people I didn't know, and that was how it was going to be for the rest of my life. It was time to get on with it.

Mrs. Avery let each of us choose what we were going to work on. She didn't make us all do the same thing or insist that we work together. Not that first day, anyway. Clive worked on a coloring book, his face almost touching it and his tongue sticking out in concentration. Michele drew a vase of daffodils that Mrs. Avery had on her desk. Roger had a book with special letters that he could read with his fingers. I sat in the corner and read a rather creepy story about a girl who punishes the family next door for killing ducks.

While I was reading I watched the others without letting them see that I was watching them. I wondered if they could ever turn into friends. The only friend I'd ever had was Justin, and that was only because our parents were friends. He was nice to me, but we were not equals. Friends should be equals.

The bell rang for lunch. I waited to see what would happen next.

"Out you go," said Mrs. Avery. "You all brought your lunch, didn't you? Everyone eats outside unless it's raining."

We'd only been in that room for a couple of hours but already I didn't want to leave it. The other kids, the normal kids, would be outside as well. Roger and Michele looked unhappy. Clive didn't mind. We shuffled silently along the corridor, me on my sticks. I got myself into my wheelchair at the door. We had still barely spoken to each other. I was wary about trying to talk to them, with my slow speaking that no one understood at first. They walked single file, Michele in front, to a bench at the side of the playground. Heads down, as though they were trying to be invisible. If it hadn't been for me and my wheelchair following them it might have worked.

We were unwrapping our sandwiches when it started.

From across the playground I heard someone shouting, "Hey, look!" A boy separated himself from the clump of kids he was playing with and came toward us. Some of the others followed him. The boy was about my age, but big and strong. "Who are you lot, then? "

None of us said anything.

"I know who you are," he said. "You're the cripples. Who do you think you are, coming to our school? Eh? Who asked you to come?"

We stared back, mute and frozen.

"What, you can't talk either? Crippled and dumb, eh?"

I glanced at Michele and Roger and Clive. Clive looked puzzled. The others were expressionless.

"My dad says you should go to your own school. We don't want any morons here."

Roger flinched as though he'd been hit.

"Go away," Michele said to the boy. "Leave us alone."

He took a step towards her and stood right over her. "Pardon me? What did you say, chickenlegs?" He kicked her calliper.

Michele gasped. "Nothing! I didn't say anything!"

"Adam!" It was a man's voice. "Adam Widmer! Get away from there!" I turned and saw one of the teachers I'd noticed in the morning, a man with a yellow shirt and a brown tie.

"I wasn't doing anything, sir. Just wanted to meet the new children."

"Well, now you've met them, get back to your side of the playground."

Adam gave us a rude, slow look and sauntered back to his friends. The teacher paid no more attention to us.

I stared at the ground. My heart was whizzing like a racecar and my mouth was dry. I wanted to say sorry, I'm really sorry I made him notice us. I wanted to ask Michele if her leg was hurting. It was one of those times when it was particularly awful not to be able to talk properly.

"He's wrong," said Michele. "We're not morons. And we're allowed to be here."

"Just ignore him," said Roger. "My mother said that's what we should do if people tease us."

We all nodded. What else could we do?

When lunchtime was over I thought the others would tell Mrs. Avery what happened. But they said nothing, and Mrs. Avery didn't ask. I felt too shy to tell her myself. I hoped that the boy would leave us alone, now that he'd told us how he felt.

At the end of the day my mother came to take me home. I saw Michele limping out of the schoolyard. No one walked with her, but I didn't see anyone teasing her either.

My mother wanted to know all about the day. As best I could, I told her about the others in the class, and what we had done in school. I did not mention Adam, the mean boy.

The next day it was raining at lunchtime and we all stayed inside. I was relieved, and the others seemed to be too. There was suddenly a good mood in the room, everyone laughing and making fun of what their mothers put in their sandwiches but gobbling them up anyway. Michele gave me one of her chocolate biscuits. I gave her half of the orange that my mother had cut up for me.

On Wednesday the sun was out. As lunchtime approached my stomach started lurching as though it was spastic too. I thought about telling Mrs. Avery that I wasn't feeling well and needed to stay inside. But if Michele and Roger and Clive were brave enough to go out, I'd have to go too.

For a while it was fine because Adam was on the other side of the playground, playing a chasing game with some other boys. But after a few minutes he noticed us. He stopped the game and came over. The other boys came with him. They stood over us. I could smell their clothes and the mud on their shoes. Their knees were scratched and grubby from their game.

"I thought I told you we didn't want you here," he said.

"Yeah," said one of his friends. "You don't belong in our school."

"I'm warning you," said Adam. "You'd better go back to idiot school, if you don't want to get hurt."

We sneaked desperate glances at each other. If they wanted to hurt us, what could we do?

They crowded around us. I stared down at their feet, bracing myself for a kick from one of those heavy lace-up shoes. Then they turned and left. I held tight to the arms of my chair, suddenly afraid I would slither out of it.

"My mum told me that some of the other families didn't want us to come here," said Michele. "She said we have to be patient. They'll get used to us."

For a few days Adam and his friends were occupied with playing football. A couple of times they shouted rude names as they ran by but they didn't come and threaten us again.

When we weren't worrying about them it was nice to be outside, eating our lunches. Michele told us about her village school, where there were only seven children, tiny ones and older ones. The teacher spent most of her time with the babies and let the older kids do what they wanted. "It was fun," said Michele. "But I wasn't learning anything."

The next week Adam and the others came back.

"Still here?" he said. "Well then, what have you got for me?"

We stared at him. What did he mean?

"What have you got for me, chickenlegs?" he said again to Michele. "Ooh, thank you, don't mind if I do." He grabbed Michele's ginger biscuits and ate one, then offered them to his friends, who finished them in a second. Michele stared down at the ground.

"What about you, spit-and-dribble?" Adam said to me. "Yes, you. Look at me when you're spoken to." He kicked my chair. "You got anything for me?" I would have given him anything so that he'd leave me alone. But I'd already finished my lunch.

He picked up my empty crisps bag and shook it, then leaned down and breathed in my face. I smelt the sandwich he'd just had, ham and mustard. "You'd better bring me one of these tomorrow or you'll be sorry." He kicked my chair again, and one of the other boys kicked it too. "Yeah," echoed the other boy. His name was Brian. He looked like Adam, but thinner and not so red-cheeked. "You'll be sorry."

"Come on," said Adam, "let's play again before the bell rings." They ran off.

The other kids were silent. Then I realized that Michele was crying and trying not to.

"Don't cry," said Clive. "Do you want my sweet?" He handed her a toffee.

"Let's tell Mrs. Avery," I said, or my rendition of it. The others looked doubtful, but when we went inside Michele and Roger came with me to talk to her. Clive didn't really understand. We let him get on with his coloring books.

Mrs. Avery frowned and shook her head. "What a shame," she said. "What rude and unkind behavior. Let me see. Tomorrow, when you go outside, I'll come with you. Good idea?"

We thought it was an excellent idea. And it worked, until she got up and went back inside to have her own lunch in the teachers' room. As soon as she was out of sight the boys came over again, teasing us about needing our teacher to look after us, grabbing our lunch boxes to see if anything was left.

We looked at each other when the bell rang and Adam and his friends ran back to their own classrooms.

"Do you think they'll get tired of it?" asked Michele.

"Maybe," I said, though I didn't think they'd stop unless someone made them. They were having a lot of fun teasing us.

We told Mrs. Avery again when we went inside. "Oh dear," she said. "The thing is that this is so new for everyone. I'm sorry to say that some of the parents objected to having handicapped children at Eastcott. I know it's not fair. But it'll change. Just try to be brave and ignore them. They're not really hurting you, are they?"

She wanted us to agree, so we did. But it wasn't true. Adam had kicked Michele's leg. He and his friends hurt our feelings by making us all scared and ashamed.

"No one can really help," said Michele when we went back to our desks. "It's because we're handicapped."

Roger nodded.

I told my mother I wanted a bit more for my lunch, some extra crisps and biscuits.

"School makes you hungry, doesn't it!" my mother said happily. She thought it meant I was being a real schoolboy.

If I managed not to think about Adam, I liked being a schoolboy. I liked coming to the school each day, seeing the other kids, seeing Mrs. Avery, finding out what she'd planned for us to do that day. We each had different things that we liked and wanted to learn more about. Michele loved art. I didn't. It was too hard for me to manage a paintbrush or even a crayon. But I liked watching Michele. One day she drew a portrait of me, with charcoal. She didn't draw the wheelchair, just me. Mrs. Avery pinned it up on the wall. It looked like me, but not pathetic or stupid.

What I was good at was reading books and making up stories and poems. Mrs. Avery had a typewriter in the classroom and I was learning how to use it. The clinic gave me little weights for my wrists so that my hands didn't float around so much when I typed. It was much better than trying to write with a pen or pencil. It still took me a long time, but once I'd finished Mrs. Avery would read it aloud. It was wonderful, hearing my words flowing along in her voice. She put some of my stories up on the wall, too.

Outside on the playground each day was different. We never knew what to expect. We braced ourselves for terrifying visits from the mean boys, but sometimes they ignored us, if they had something more exciting to do. Those days were almost worse than the bullying days, because we knew that sooner or later they'd bully us again. We could never just think about our lunch, or our conversation.

I noticed that the teachers outside at lunchtime knew what was going on. They didn't try very hard to stop it. One of them, Mr. Stratton, looked at my wheelchair and shook his head. "This is what happens when children like you insist on coming to an ordinary school," he said, after sending Adam to the other side of the playground.

Going to school, as I said, was the first shock. The second one came a month or two later. My mother had just brought me home, tired and messy from the school day. She cleaned me up, as usual, and sat with me in the living room.

"Tell me about school today," she said, as she always did. I started to tell her—my usual partial account, leaving out anything that would worry her—but she wasn't listening. "Your father will be back very soon," she said, glancing at her watch.

I didn't know why that was worth mentioning since he was usually back around then unless he had drama club or a teachers' meeting. We heard the front door open and close, and the sounds of him taking off his jacket in the hallway and hanging it up. When he came in I saw a glance between them like a little silver arrow. He sat next to her on the couch and put his hand on hers.

"Alex, we have some lovely news to tell you," said my father.

It was a bit like when my mum told me about going to school: they weren't at all sure how I would take this lovely news. My stomach immediately started rolling over.

"Your mother is going to have a baby."

My mother looked up at him and then at me, her cheeks suddenly pink. I listened to his words echoing in my mind, waiting for them to land somewhere in my brain. A baby. I felt like my wheels were on the edge of a cliff. A baby. I was a baby too. I didn't want to be, but I couldn't help it. With a real baby, how could they take care of me? I wanted to cry but I knew that it would be a very bad idea. So I forced myself to smile and nod in my wobbly way. My mother knelt in front of me, holding the arms of my chair. She leaned forward and kissed my cheek.

"We're so pleased, Alex," she said. "Soon you'll be a big brother." She sat down again, close to my father. He patted her tummy. I saw that it was big and round and I was surprised that I hadn't noticed before. I stared at it, imagining a miniature person curled up under my mother's brown dress, its eyes tightly shut. I didn't know whether to picture a crippled baby or a normal baby. My mother looked at me, at my aimless arms and feeble legs. There was a little shadow in her eyes and I knew she was wondering too.

That night I woke up in tears. I was ashamed but I couldn't stop myself. I thought about the baby who was coming, and I thought how much my parents would love that little child who would be able to do all the things that I couldn't do, who would be sweet and funny and bright, and would make ordinary baby noises, and then talk, and walk, and go to school when he was five years old, and run and shout on the playground with the other kids. And I thought that my mother and father would love this little boy so much that they wouldn't want to look after me any more. They wouldn't have time to read books with me and help me eat and get dressed and go to the toilet and take me for my therapy every week. They'd want to be like the other families, going to the market, going to the beach, playing games in the park. All those things that families did, that we couldn't do, because of me. They would probably need to send me away. My mother had told me that when I was born I almost died and now I wished that I had, instead surviving in a body that didn't work.

My crying was quiet, I know it was—I couldn't make a lot of sound even if I wanted to—but my mother heard and came in. She lay down beside me and held me. For a while she didn't say anything. I could feel the big hard lump of her belly. She murmured my name. After a while, when I calmed down, she raised herself on her elbow and looked at me. I could just see her face in the light of the street lamp outside.

"Francis really wanted another baby, Alex. It's been hard. You know." Of course things were hard. Life was hard when you had a crippled kid. It wasn't until much later that I understood what she meant: my parents thought that another baby, a healthy baby, might make things better between them. And it did, for a while.

I looked at her, then rolled onto my other side.

"Don't be scared," she said, stroking my back in the dark. "You're our firstborn. Nothing can change that."

Not long after that I had a grand mal seizure for the first time. In the morning I had waited with increasing dread for whatever torments Adam and his pals might think up. By lunchtime I'd worked myself into a state of terror.

"Come on, Alex," said Mrs. Avery, cross with me when minutes went by and I had not done a single arithmetic problem. "You can do better than that." But all I could do was watch the big round clock with its cruel hands jerking closer and closer to noon. As soon as we went outside the boys surrounded us, picking over our lunches for treats to steal. We let them. We had no choice. When they left without actually hurting any of us we pretended everything was fine. But it wasn't.

I was more than tired than usual when I came home. I tried to lift my head to answer my mother when she asked me about the day. Her voice sounded far away. I could hardly hear what she was saying through the humming in my ears. The light looked different, brighter, glassy somehow. I could hear her shouting "Alex! Alex!" from a great distance and then I fell down into a dark, dark cave.

When I opened my eyes again I was on the floor with a blanket over me. My mother was crouching awkwardly beside me, with her big belly. My father hovered behind her. They both looked afraid. My mother stroked my head very gently. "Alex. How do you feel?" She told me I'd had a seizure. She recognized what was happening—people with cerebral palsy often get seizures, sooner or later. She phoned Dr. Barrow while I lay there twitching and jerking for ten minutes. "Just keep him quiet and warm," he said. "Bring him in when he's calmed down." She'd telephoned my father and asked him to hurry home with the car.

I did not have enough strength to sit up after the seizure. I felt confused and my head hurt badly. "A couple of days at home and he'll be right as rain," advised the doctor after looking me over. He told my parents that I'd probably been having little seizures for years, but with someone like me it would be hard to notice.

Once I felt better I did not want to go back to school. The little bit of courage that I'd been able to dredge up to face the bullies each day had gone. I tried to think about all the things I liked—being friends with Michele and Clive and Roger, reading and writing, playing the games that Mrs. Avery thought up for us at the end of each day. But it was no use.

I managed to put it off for a few more days, letting my mother think I was still feeling poorly. But then she started getting bossy.

"Come on, Alex, time to get up," she said one morning, pulling up the blinds in my room with a snap. "Back to school today."

I burrowed down into my bed. "I'm not going!" I hardly ever refused to do what she wanted but this felt like life and death.

My mother stopped rummaging in my sock drawer and came over to the bed. She sat down.

"What's going on, Alex?"

I couldn't resist her gentle voice. So I told her.

It made her cry. She kept asking why I had never told her before, until finally she seemed to understand that I just couldn't. She let me stay at home again that day, and in the evening we all talked about it, she and my father and I.

He listened to her—I begged her to tell him what I'd said, so I didn't have to say it all again—with shock on his face, and then he jumped up and smacked the wall. "What the hell is wrong with those kids? And their parents?" He paced to the front window and back. "How can the school let this go on?" He was cross with himself and my mother too. "Maybe we pushed too hard, Naomi," he said. "Westerford is apparently not ready after all."

"And give up on Alex's right to an education?" said my mother. "Those families are just the rear guard, Francis. Some people hate change."

"What those kids need is a good punch in the face," he said. "Teach them a lesson. That's what I did when some lads tried to pick on me when I was at school. They left me alone after that."

"Thanks, Francis, that's very helpful," said my mother, flashing her eyes at him.

My father squatted down in front of my chair. "Sorry, son. No one should ever treat you like that. Ever. Are you going to be OK?"

I nodded. I hated being such a feeble, pathetic person. I would have liked very much to punch Adam.

"The best thing to do is ignore it," said my dad. "They just want to see you get upset."

Everyone seemed to think the bullies would stop if we ignored them. We already knew it didn't work.

"What about the other kids?" said my mother. "The normal kids? Do they stick up for you?"

"They don't," I said. "They're scared of Adam too."

My mother and father argued about what to do. My dad wanted to phone Adam's parents immediately. He'd never met them but Adam's father was the owner of the largest car dealership in Westerford. My mother thought it would make things worse for me, and I agreed. "We'll talk to Miss Hetherington," she said. "She absolutely has to know." That worried me too. If the headmistress punished Adam and Brian and the others, they'd just take it out on us.

"Look, we have to do something, Alex," said my mother. "You can't stay at home forever because of this young lout."

The next day she rang all the parents of my classmates. They came to our house a couple of evenings later, Miss Hetherington as well. Michele came with her mother. She and I sat listening to the grown-ups, who asked us questions from time to time: yes, it was mostly Adam and his friends, though other children sometimes called us names or made fun of how we looked or walked or spoke. Yes, some children were friendly. A few of the teachers tried to help but others didn't. Yes, we liked going to Eastcott, in spite of the bullying. We liked Mrs. Avery. We liked each other.

The grown-ups sat silent, thinking.

"Every school has bullies," said Miss Hetherington at last. "I'm afraid having special kids just gives them a handy target."

"But there must be something you can do!" said Michele's mother, scowling. "Surely!" Her hair was untidy, as though she didn't remember to brush it. She kept smoking cigarettes, not noticing that my mother did not like it.

Miss Hetherington stared at a stain on the living room wall. I always thought it looked like a ship. She seemed younger than any of the parents. She sighed and shook her head.

"All right. I'll talk to Adam and his henchmen tomorrow. And I'll remind the teachers that they are obliged to stop cruelty whenever they see it. But I can't change human nature." She turned to us. "Alex and Michele. I'm proud of you and the others. You're like pioneers. One day all schools will welcome handicapped kids, and you'll have helped to make that happen. For now…" She paused. "For now, you have to be strong. I know you can do it."

I felt strong when I heard her say that, and proud, too. We could put up with some bullying if we were pioneers.

CHAPTER FOUR

August 30, 1997, afternoon

They drive slowly through the Bois, still blessedly free of the hyenas. The oak woods and ponds and gardens remind her of the parklands around her childhood home, where she played in freedom with her brother or alone--no spies in the trees, no hidden cameras with telephoto lenses. Two young girls on ponies trot across the road, the girls in jodhpurs and riding hats, neat and serious, their chestnut ponies gleaming. She remembers Bibby, her own pony, not nearly so handsome or well groomed. Bibby would take her anywhere and graze contentedly if she wanted to lie on the grass and read in the sun for a while, or have a picnic of bread and cheese and cake by the stream.

The sun through the car window warms her skin, in spite of the air-conditioning. She could close her eyes and drowse. She leans against her lover, regretful now about her irritation in the villa. He encircles her with his arm and kisses her neck. "We must spend more time in Paris," he says. "When the boys go back to school." She nods, though she knows she will not come back soon. And when she does, it will not be to see him. She has been deliberately vague about what will happen between them, to spare his feelings. But he is not part of her future. Her future! She lets herself daydream again about the new threshold that she hopes is in front of her. She is impatient to hear from Hugh, who should have news by now.

They approach a little carousel, twirling gaily with small children clinging to their mounts. She lowers the car window to hear the jubilant music. A woman pushes a small wheelchair towards the enclosure. A mother? A nurse? Is she going to try to lift that child onto the carousel? How the child would love it, the music and movement, up and down, round and round. The exhilaration. But perhaps they're just there to watch.

She would like to pause and see what happens, but the car keeps moving and the carousel is out of sight. She rests her head on the back of the seat and closes her eyes again, then suddenly stiffens. A car is beside them, blocking the sun. "They've found us!" she cries.

But it's only a driver in a hurry. He speeds past and disappears.

"Don't worry," her lover soothes her. "We're safe."

CHAPTER FIVE

Alex

Michele's mother was the caretaker at a manor house in a village outside Westerford. The first time I went to visit, Michele showed me around the whole house. The living room—"the drawing room," corrected Michele—was twice as big as our whole downstairs. It had pillars and a marble fireplace. The owners lived in London, two hundred miles away, and came for occasional weekends. The room was freezing cold. We wrapped ourselves in the soft patterned rugs that hung over the backs of couches.

"They pretend that they're toffs, but they're not, they're just ordinary people who make pots of money doing PR," said Michele.

I didn't know what PR was.

"Making people famous, that's what PR is. Public relations."

"What?" I said. "How can you make someone famous?" Either you were famous or you weren't.

"They could make us famous," said Michele. She put on a BBC voice. "Channel Four presents: 'HANDICAPPED! The True Story of Alex, Michele, and the Bully!'"

I thought that might make a good story. It would have a happy ending, with Adam getting told off and us living free of him forever.

The rooms where Michele and her mother, Jane, lived were small and low ceilinged, with moisture running down the walls. They'd been the servants' quarters in the old days. I liked Jane. She didn't want me to call her Mrs. Ferguson. She said it was debatable whether she was Mrs. Anyone, since Michele's dad was in the merchant navy and hardly ever came home any more. Jane was a stocky, round-shouldered woman, always smoking. Her short blond-grey hair often had dried paint in it because she was an artist and when she was trying to sort out a painting problem she'd throw down her brush and rub her head with both hands.

"All right," Jane said one day when my mother had dropped us off after school. "You can watch for fifteen minutes, as long as you don't talk."

She stared out the window, her eyes narrowed. She rubbed her head hard, then picked up a brush and made a stroke on the canvas, stepped back, looked, made another one. A shape slowly emerged from streaks and blobs of color. I wasn't sure what it was but it made me want to keep looking. It made me want to walk right into the painting.

We tiptoed out after a few minutes. "People sometimes came here to buy her paintings," Michele told me. "Not that often. But they pay a lot of money."

I was impressed. I wasn't at all good at art. But I liked looking at my parents' art books. My London grandmother, my mother's mum, had given me two Salvador Dali prints and they hung in my room. I told Jane about them, and she was polite, but I could tell that she did not admire Salvador Dali.

The baby arrived one day while I was at school. My dad came to fetch me home instead of my mother. He was sending off sparks of excitement. As soon as we were out of the school grounds he crouched down in front of my chair. "Guess what, Alex!" he said, and I knew right away that the baby had come. I cried out with excitement, almost missing what he said next: "You have a little sister!"

A sister! It hadn't occurred to me that the baby might be a girl. I liked the idea very much. He laughed and hugged me. "Let's go and see them!" We drove up the hill to the new maternity hospital with fields and cows beside it. The lift took us up to a hallway painted in bright colors. Women walked along in their dressing gowns with huge tight tummies in front of them, or cuddling wrapped-up bundles.

My mother was in a bed with one of those bundles. She was very pale, but she looked happy to see us. "Come and meet your baby sister, Alex!"

My dad pushed my chair up to the side of the bed.

"This is Gillian." She held out the bundle so I could see it. "Gillian, this is your brother."

Her face was extremely small, like a doll's face, and red. Her eyes were tight shut but as I watched she opened them slowly and looked at me. My father took her and put her in my lap, very gently. I wrapped my arms around her. I didn't know a human being could be so small. "Gillian," I said. I felt she could understand me.

Gillian was normal. Everyone was very happy about that, though before she was born no one, at least in my hearing, had said out loud that they were worried. But she was beautiful and perfect. I heard them say it a million times, not just my parents but my London grandparents, the neighbors, everyone. My mother sent a photo to my Northumberland grandmother, my dad's mother. A parcel arrived from her with a little smocked dress and a note saying she'd like to come and see the baby. Thrilled though he was with his pretty little girl, my father refused. "She had her chance," he said. I'd heard by then about his mother's visit when I was a year old, not to admire and cuddle me but to tell my parents to put me in a home and have another baby right away. A replacement.

Gillian didn't replace me. She made our family complete. I was very proud of my baby sister. If I couldn't be beautiful and perfect at least I could be the brother of someone who was.

Adam Widmer was not the only bully at our school and we were not his only targets. But he specialized in us. We were his preferred victims. His personal cripples. After Miss Hetherington talked to him he left us alone for a couple of weeks. But then he started up again. I suppose we got used to it, the way you can get used to anything no matter how painful. I noticed other kids being teased, hit, shamed, left out, sometimes by Adam, sometimes by other boys and girls. They weren't handicapped but there was usually something about them that others picked on—they had red hair, or glasses, or they weren't good at games, or they were fat, or poor, or their mother had left their father. Or they were just different in some way that was hard to pinpoint but unmistakable, marking them like a smell they could not get rid of. I felt sorry for them.

Teachers could be cruel too. "Pull yourself together, lad," said Mr. Stratton to Roger. "No one likes a sissy." Roger was crying because Brian and Adam had enticed him out onto the playground and then let him walk into the fence. Those teachers seemed to think that bullying was good for you. Bracing, like a swim in a freezing river. Sometimes a teacher would scold Adam in a joking way that told him—and me, watching—that the teacher actually admired his boldness. Adam was very good at games and even I could see that he was good-looking, with thick hair and bright brown eyes. Grown-ups liked him.

Michele and I wondered a lot about Adam, why he was so mean, especially when no one was mean to him. He had lots of pals. Girls wanted to be his girlfriend. But he seemed to enjoy being horrible.

"Do you think he has cruel parents?" I asked Michele. We were at my house, minding the baby while my mother went to the shops. Gillian was six months old. She had wispy dark hair and merry eyes and she knew how to sit up already. She smiled and made funny noises. She thought she was talking, like us. I loved her more than anyone or anything in the world. We sat on the floor, playing with her. If we did something silly Gillian would laugh out loud. That was our reward.

Michele shrugged. "Maybe he's just got bad blood."

Gillian flopped forward onto her knees and shuffled forward a few inches.

"Look!" I yelled. "She's crawling!" Already she'd done things that I'd never learned how to do. I was so proud of her.

Michele leaned down and kissed the baby's cheek. "Clever girlie! Clever girlie!"

Adam discovered that it was fun to persuade us that he wasn't a bully any more, that he really wanted to be friends. Michele never fell for it but at one time or another the rest of us did. Clive was so pleased about everything that it wasn't easy to upset him, but Adam succeeded. He pretended to admire the daisies and dandelions that Clive had just picked. When Clive let him hold the flowers, Adam dropped them and stepped on them—"Oh dear! Clumsy me." Clive's constant smile froze on his face. He wept. Adam's friends backed away, leaving him alone with his triumph.

My turn came on a cool, cloudy day in March when I'd been at Eastcott for almost a school year. By then I was eleven. After the summer holidays we'd all go to secondary school. If I thought about it when I woke up during the night I couldn't get back to sleep. By now I knew that I was as good at schoolwork as most of the other kids. But being bright isn't nearly enough to survive.

After a couple of days without Adam's attentions he waved at me from the group of kids he was playing with, and came over. I braced myself.

"Hello, Alex," he said, smiling affably. He'd never called me anything but spit-and-dribble before. I didn't think he even knew my name. "Listen, I know you really like reading and all, don't you? You're a real swot!" He said it with admiration. In Mrs. Avery's room everyone knew I loved reading and writing, and I was quite good at it. Sometimes I let myself daydream about getting top marks in the end of year exam. Maybe I'd get the English prize. How surprised everyone would be that a handicapped kid who couldn't talk properly could win the English prize.

So there was a part of me that was ready to believe Adam's flattery.

"Do you think you could help me with my English homework?" He pulled a funny face and rolled his eyes. "I'm going to get into trouble if I don't hand it in today. Know what I mean?"

I couldn't help nodding sympathetically.

"My book's over there," he said, pointing. "It'd just take a couple of minutes."

I nodded OK. In an instant I forgot about Adam's cruelty and thought only about the heady possibility of being friends with him. A friend who was a normal boy, someone that others looked up to and obeyed. Everything would be different if I had an ally like that. And why shouldn't someone like Adam want to be friends with me?

These mad thoughts bloomed in a split second. I ignored the others looking at me with alarm. If they were as clever as me, I thought in my delusion, Adam might make friends with them too.

He wheeled me toward the benches on the other side of the playground. I hoped everyone was watching—me and my friend Adam, smiling and chatting together. His pals were waiting. It was like arriving in a different country. I looked back at Michele, Roger and Clive and saw how isolated and pathetic they looked in our little spot by the yew hedge.

"Here," said Adam still in his friendly tone. "Here's the book." But it was a magazine he held up in front of me, not a book at all. The cover had a picture of a naked woman with huge breasts. I looked at it, confused.

"Ever seen tits like those?" said Brian. He stroked them with his finger. "Ooh, yeah, baby."

"Show him the cock," said Adam. Brian flipped through some pages, then held the magazine in front of my face. I saw another naked girl sprawled on a bed and a man standing in front of her with a huge penis. The boys guffawed. "Just like yours, eh, spit-and-dribble? Want to show us?" said Adam. Terror throttled me. I thought they were going to pull down my shorts. I had to get away. How utterly, unbelievably stupid

I'd been to let Adam trick me. I turned my wheelchair, expecting them to grab it any second.

"Got you all excited, eh?" said Adam. "Off you go, have a wank in the bushes."

I wheeled myself back across the playground with agonizing slowness, their taunting voices following me. About half way Michele and Clive came to meet me and pushed my chair back to our bench. They said nothing, and nor did I.

Lunchtime was over. We went back inside. Mrs. Avery took out her guitar to play some songs with us, which I usually enjoyed, but today I was unable to listen at all. I was too upset about what had happened, Adam's fake friendliness, my stupidity in falling for it, the nasty magazine. I saw my mother without her clothes sometimes, and my dad too. I liked seeing their strong bodies. The people in the magazine looked nothing like them. I didn't really understand about sex. My father had told me the basics about how boys and girls develop, how women get pregnant. I knew that older kids and grown-ups talked about sex a lot. There seemed to be a lot of danger and excitement around it. That was the part I didn't get, but it didn't worry me. It didn't seem to have much to do with me.

Summer came and school ended. We said goodbye to Mrs. Avery. She told us that she'd have a new group of handicapped pupils in September. "It was you who paved the way," she said. "I've learned so much from all of you." She hugged each of us. "Come back and visit Eastcott some time."

Michele was jubilant. "No more school! No more you-know-who!" she crowed when Jane took us to get ice cream cornets on the Strand. Jane had to help me with mine or it would have ended up on my face or the ground. I ignored the stares of two little girls who were making a mess of their own ice creams. Michele and I were going to play together all through the summer. I didn't have to be alone the way I used to be.

One day in August she pushed me outside to the old walled garden at the back of the manor house. You could still see the raised rows where they had grown vegetables for the huge old kitchen. A fig tree stretched out its arms along the sun-warmed stone. We ate raspberries from overgrown bushes. Michele had been very quiet all afternoon. I was waiting for her to tell me what was wrong. We leaned against the warm wall, Michele sitting on the ground, me in the wheelchair.

"You're lucky you're not a girl," she said after a while. Her head was bent and her hair hid her face.

"Why?"

"I loathe Dr. Barrow." We both went to Dr. Barrow for our check ups and our health problems. I didn't like him much. Michele had had an appointment the day before.

"What did he do?"

"How would he like it?" Michele turned to me furiously. "How do you think he'd like to walk up and down with nothing on and tons of people staring and poking and squeezing you?"

"How many people? Who were they?" I was trying to make sense of what she was saying.

"I don't know, a lot. Four, maybe. Plus him. Five men. No one asked me if they could, did they?"

It sounded awful. I was trying to understand. "But why?"

"And all those rude questions!"

"Like what?"

"It was so embarrassing. Absolutely none of their business."

Her head was down again. Her shoulders shook. I wanted to murder Dr. Barrow.

"Where was your mum?" I asked.

"She left me there. We thought it was just an ordinary check up."

I didn't know what to say. I reached down and patted her shoulder as best I could. She let me do this for a moment, then clambered to her feet.

"Let's go around the front." She pushed me along the brick pathway that surrounded the house. Sheep grazed in the green fields that sloped down towards Westerford, visible in the distance. Michele was trying hard to collect herself. She didn't want me to look at her. I watched the sheep.

"How come they don't come right up here and eat the flowers?"

"Because of the haha."

I didn't know what she was talking about. She wheeled me across the lawn. From the house the lawn appeared to continue smoothly into the fields beyond. But the ground abruptly dropped about four feet, creating a barrier that the sheep couldn't climb.

"See? That's called a haha."

"Haha," I repeated. It was such a silly name. It must have come from laughing at someone who tripped on it.

Michele lay on the ground with her legs hanging over the haha. After a moment I slid out of my wheelchair and lay down beside her. The grass was warm and springy under my back.

"Do you know what the worst thing was, Alex?"

"No."

"He said I would probably never have children. Bear children, he said."

With an effort I rolled onto my side and looked at her. "He told you that?"

"They weren't talking to me, were they? He said it to the other doctors or whatever they were. 'This patient is unlikely ever to bear children.'" Michele imitated his posh voice. "I was standing right there. I'm not an idiot! I'm not deaf!"

I thought that was a particularly unkind thing for Dr. Barrow to say. Michele liked babies. She wanted to get married one day and have at least two kids, she said. A boy and a girl. Sometimes she drew pictures of them. She even had names picked out, Karl and Karen.

I didn't believe Dr. Barrow anyway. How could he know something like that? "This is what I say to him," I said. "HAHA to you, Dr. Barrow! HAHA!"

I reached out my hand and grasped hers. It felt small and warm and strong. "Hahaha," we yelled down the green fields to Westerford. Hahaha, Dr. Barrow and all the people who treat us like freaks.

CHAPTER SIX

August 30, 1997, afternoon

By the time they reach the Ritz, the pack has found them again. Tall men surround them as they leave the car, employees of his father, who owns the hotel. They are charged with the impossible task of providing privacy and protection. She looks past the burly shoulders of the bodyguards and catches the eye of one of the photographers, who hails her as though they were old friends and snaps a volley of rapid shots before she escapes through the gleaming gilt doors of the hotel. In the elevator up to her lover's suite, high above the busy boulevard, he embraces her as though they were alone. "We'll rest, mon amour. Later, some music, yes? Some dinner?" The bodyguards stare at the changing numbers of the floors as though the most glamorous couple in the world is not kissing in front of them.

The rooms are enormous and quiet. Vases of white roses and orchids. Three bottles of champagne in a huge silver cooler. The guards leave them at the door. They are alone again. They lie down on quilted pale blue silk, but he is restless.

"I'll be back, darling. Enjoy yourself."

She manages a small smile. He seems to be intent on something, one of his ingratiating surprises. She has no idea what and doesn't care. As soon as he is gone she tries Hugh again on the hotel room phone. He's told her not to use her mobile, too easily hacked, as she knows all too well. "You've reached British Telecom's automated answering service," chirps the recorded voice. Hugh is too cautious to have a personal greeting on his phone. She doesn't leave another message. He'll phone her back if he has news.

The day is passing too slowly. Only a few hours left, and then she will go home. She amuses herself with the things that usually comfort her, a team of hairdressers, an expert massage. She lies still under the masseur's skillful hands. They feel kind, those hands. She is grateful, though aware that it is purchased kindness. Has anyone in her life ever shown her true kindness?

She had thought, for a while, that her lover and his father were kind. They cradled her bruised self in their family warmth, comforting her, flattering her, giving her a haven, at least for a while. She relaxed and flowered with their attentions, feeling loved and safe.

She had never felt loved and safe in her husband's family. Never. Even at their most private it was not possible to simply relax and take pleasure in each other's company. There was, instead, a dense and invisible web of rules, hundreds of years of rules waiting to be shattered by the gauche foot of an outsider. They had no idea how cruel they were, how medieval. She remembered the grandmother, over one of those interminable teas during the engagement, talking in her soft, relentless voice about carrying on the monarchy, what a solemn responsibility it was, how important to be certain that one was worthy and ready. She had listened, murmuring agreement, unsure where this was leading but thrilled with the sense of history and destiny, the humbling honor of being chosen as a vessel.

Then a few days later the consultation in the rooms of the royal gynecologist. He was cordial enough, though formal. Too patrician himself to wear a white coat. He sat behind his desk in his elegant suit asking her the most personal questions about her menstruation, any diseases or infections, her mother and sisters and their reproductive history. He asked about previous boyfriends—had there been penetration? He wrote down her barely audible responses, not looking at her scarlet face. Then he told her to undress, and probed the contours and cavities of her body while she lay stretched out on the examining table like a cadaver in a laboratory.

He reported to his employers—she was told later—that she was magnificently ready for childbearing and yes, intact. It was only much later, years later, that she let herself hear the suppressed voice within her that had wanted to shriek, to the doctor, to the grandmother, to the promiscuous prince and his parents: How dare you?

Lying on the massage table she shudders.

The masseur pauses. "Are you cold, your Highness?"

"No, I'm all right. Thank you."

He continues the stroke. He doesn't know, she thinks, that they stripped me of "Her Royal Highness" a year ago, punishment for my wicked ways. I don't care what they call me. I hardly know what to call myself.

She knew by now that her lover's father had his own plans. He had offered her as a trophy to his charming, clueless son—an instrument of revenge against those who had humiliated him, who had refused to admit him, in spite of his fabled wealth, to the table of the truly elite. Thick as a plank, she once claimed about herself, and yet she was smart enough to discern that he was rubbing his hands at the thought of a wedding and then children who would be of his blood. A devastating slap in the royal face. His son wasn't capable of such ambition. For him she was simply the shiniest of all his shiny and expensive acquisitions.

She was dozing again on the pale silk when he came in.

"Wake up, darling! Look what I brought you!"

She remembers her boys, on holiday in Spain: "Wake up, Mummy! Look what we brought you!" and she opened her eyes to a tray of boy-made breakfast.

Her lover holds out a black velvet jewel box. She opens it, exclaiming delight, as she knows he expects. The necklace is spectacular, befitting his father's son. "And there's a ring, too," he says, eager. "They're fixing the size." Alarmed, she wonders if he's about to propose. It would be absurd. They are nothing more than ciphers for each other, a handsome man for her, a beautiful woman for him, of more or less the right age and size.

CHAPTER SEVEN

Alex

I'm lucky. In my life I have not met many unkind people. But I've met a few, and Adam Widmer was the worst by far. And yet, in a strange way, a terrible way, it was because of him that I met Diana. That's the way it goes, I suppose. I don't think he'd even remember who I was. Though I imagine he remembers Michele. If he doesn't, he's even worse than I thought.

The local grammar school, where my father taught until he finally left to be a university lecturer at Exeter, had recently become a comprehensive. Everyone said it was the best school to go in Westerford if you were clever. Unless you were also handicapped. They'd never had handicapped pupils before and the headmaster did not want to take me.

"We won't be able to make any special provisions," warned Mr. Shawcroft, the headmaster, when my parents spoke to him. He wouldn't have even considered it if my father was not a former teacher. "Not like Eastcott. Sink or swim with the rest of the pupils."

It made me horribly anxious but I was determined to go. Now that I knew I could manage the schoolwork reasonably well I wanted to keep learning. I'd even started thinking about university, eventually. I hadn't talked to anyone about that. I wasn't sure whether handicapped people could go. Michele wanted to stay in ordinary school as well. It was a little easier for her, with her normal speech and almost-normal walking. We said goodbye to Roger and Clive, who were going back to special schools.

The school was much bigger than Eastcott, and further from home. There was no special classroom, no Mrs. Avery. Long hallways and staircases full of big, fast-moving girls and boys. I wouldn't be able to use my wheelchair at all, which worried me, because after a few hours my arms and shoulders ached from using my crutches.

I felt like the little mermaid who wanted so badly to have two legs like a real girl that she was willing to put up with pain like knives in her feet.

The library helped. It was huge, with thousands of books sitting on their shelves just waiting for me to explore them. And on a table in the back, an electric typewriter.

"Is it..." I began. The librarian, who was showing me around, didn't wait for me to finish. "Yes, lad, it's for the pupils to use. Any time you want."

There was a blank piece of paper in it. "Go ahead, dear," said the librarian. I'd never used an electric typewriter before. The keys pushed down so easily and quietly. I saw myself writing, writing, watching my words stream onto paper, where my thoughts would go directly into other people's minds. If it took me half an hour to write a sentence, the reader would never know.

Adam had also chosen Westerford Comprehensive, with its reputation for sports as well as academics. During our first year of high school he ignored us most of the time. He had his hands full finding his own place. We were all suddenly the youngest instead of the oldest. We didn't know our way around the buildings and the grounds, we didn't know the school's complicated customs. We were self-conscious in our new uniforms, though I was relieved to wear long trousers that hid my muscle-less legs. The older pupils considered us fair game for teasing, just because we were younger and new. Michele and I got extra teasing for being handicapped, by kids our own age as well as the older ones. We didn't care very much. As long as Adam left us alone.

By the end of the first year we thought he'd forgotten about us. But we were wrong.

Adam came back after the summer holidays ready to have fun with his favorite victims again. It didn't make any sense to me. He'd been recognized as a talented football player and he was now the youngest on the school team. He'd grown tall and broad-shouldered. He had a crowd of admirers. I saw how the girls liked him. I couldn't understand why he enjoyed tormenting us so much. He kept dreaming up new ways to do it. He teased me and Michele about being boyfriend and girlfriend. We both hated it. I still looked like a kid, but Michele was changing. Her hair was cut in a new way, straight along her shoulders, with a long fringe that made her eyes dramatic even behind her glasses. Her body curved in at the waist. She had breasts. I thought she was pretty. If I'd been the kind of boy who had girlfriends, I'd have wanted her to be my girlfriend.

Michele wouldn't have wanted me as her boyfriend. I knew that. She liked a quiet boy in the third form who played the viola. She drew pictures of him in her sketchbook. He didn't know Michele existed.

Adam would try to shove me into Michele when he saw us sitting or walking together. "Go on!" he'd say. "Feel her up. Don't be scared. She's panting for it." We would freeze and shrink and wait for him to go away, then pretend it hadn't happened. It was too mortifying to talk about.

One day after school he biked past us on the river path. We were watching a fishing boat slip out with the tide. "Hey, the lovebirds," he sneered, hitting his brakes. "What a touching sight. Mr. and Mrs. Cripple. Think of all the baby cripples you'll have one day." I wished I could snap something back at him to silence him. But I couldn't think of what to say, and even if I had I couldn't have said it quickly enough.

"We're never going to get rid of him," Michele said after he'd gone with a snigger and a spray of mud from his tires.

A year later we were in the fourth form common room talking about John Lennon's new album when Adam walked past us with another boy. Everyone else adored the Beatles and hoped they would get together again, but Michele and I preferred John by himself, without the soppiness of Paul. We thought his solo songs were his best. We were not big fans of Yoko.

Adam stopped and turned back, followed by his friend. "Hey!" he said to Michele. "Lookin' sexy, chickenlegs."

Michele stared through him coldly.

"Hey, Leo, this is my old friend chickenlegs from Eastcott. We call her chickenlegs because her legs are so skinny and weird. And now chickenlegs is a sexy chick. Don't you think?"

Leo seemed embarrassed. He nodded to Michele and tried to lead Adam away. But Adam wasn't finished.

"We used to have fun at primary school, didn't we, chickenlegs? Didn't we?"

Michele said nothing.

"Answer me!" His face turned ugly and I was afraid he was going to kick her, as he used to. He put his hand on her shoulder and leaned over her, both seductive and threatening. She drew back. He spoke softly so that the other boy couldn't hear. But I could hear. "Suck me off and I won't beat you up."

I couldn't believe it.

Michele stood up. "If you don't leave me alone I'm telling the headmaster." Her voice was quiet but furious. I was proud of her.

"Come on, Adam," said his friend. Adam allowed himself to be drawn away. He looked back over his shoulder at Michele and let his tongue sag out of his mouth.

When they were gone we looked at each other. Michele had tears in her eyes.

"He's disgusting," I said. "But he can't do anything to you."

"I hate him. I. Hate. Him."

"Just ignore him. He'll get bored and leave you alone." I knew it was a dumb suggestion but I didn't know what else to say. She didn't answer.

A few days later we were making our way down the hallway in the morning, keeping to the side as usual so that the other kids could pass by us. A boy we didn't know sidled up to Michele, smirking, and held out a five pence coin. Puzzled, she looked at it, then at him. "Am I first in line?" he said. She shook her head and we kept walking. Then it happened again. This time the boy, a hulking fifth former, had a 2p coin in his hand. "That's all I got today," he said. "Enough for a bit of tongue, right?" Michele and I looked at each other with growing alarm. We were almost to our classroom when another boy stopped us. "Hey, does your pal here get a handicapped discount?" He guffawed and went on his way.

We closed the classroom door behind us. Michele was pale. "What's going on?"

But I had no idea. All I knew was that it felt awful.

Outside at lunchtime a stream of boys came over to Michele with small coins. She refused to speak to any of them or touch the coins. One held out 10p and said, "Two sucks or a fuck, ma'am." At that we fled back inside and pleaded with Miss Webb who was on hall duty to let us back in the classroom. Michele was trembling. "Why are they doing this?" she whispered, rocking herself with her arms wrapped tightly around her body. "Why? What have I done?" I made her tell Miss Webb what was happening. But she couldn't bring herself to describe the dirty suggestions and gestures that went with the coins, and to the teacher it sounded harmless, if mystifying. She was a nice enough person but she didn't understand, not at all.

"Just ignore them, dear." We'd heard that lame idea all our lives. "If you ignore them they'll get tired of it and they'll stop."

No. They wouldn't stop.

I found out what it was about when I went to the boys' toilet. Inside the stall, too high for me to reach, someone had written a two-line message in bold marker:

Chickenlegs sucks for 5p.
Shag for 10p.

I was breathless with rage. I thought I might have a seizure. I went to the headmaster's office, swinging along on my crutches so fast that I wrenched my shoulders.

"Take your time, Alex," Mr. Shawcroft said when I tried to explain what had happened. He listened until he got enough of the gist to send someone to look.

The terrible thing was that there wasn't much they could do. They cleaned the message off immediately, of course. They tried to find out who'd written it, without success. We knew. But we couldn't prove it. At assembly in the big hall Mr. Shawcroft referred to the incident carefully, saying nothing that would identify Michele as the target. He threatened expulsion to whoever was responsible, or to anyone who repeated any harmful rumors whatsoever.

But rumors don't die because they're ordered to. Adam had set something in motion that even he could not have stopped. "Five pence" became a dirty shorthand, both the word and the coin itself. Michele never knew when it would happen—a coin thrust into her hand as she waited to cross the High Street with her mother, a whisper in her ear—"Ee, five pee!"—on the bus to school, a penny taped anonymously to the back of her library book. It wasn't just boys. Some of the girls seemed to believe the rumors. "You're a slut," said one of them on the bus, a girl she'd never met before. "Disgusting, you are," said another one. "You give our school a bad name."

Adam himself went in for endless variations. He'd see Michele approaching in the corridor and when he drew alongside her he'd jingle the change in his pockets. He'd walk past as we sat outside, apparently ignoring us, then drop a coin on the ground right in front of us. "Oh dear, I think I just lost 5p, or was it ten. Did you see it?" The teachers did not suspect him at all.

Michele did not want to tell Jane and for a while I didn't argue. We had concluded with regret that parents couldn't help with bullying and might even make things worse. If they complained to the school some of the teachers would say that we were to blame because handicapped kids didn't belong there. Other teachers might be more sympathetic. But no one would do anything.

By then Michele and I had been reluctantly studying bullying for years. We were experts. We'd figured out how to put an end to it: every teacher, and most of the other parents and kids too, would have to agree that being cruel was not OK and wouldn't be permitted.

And that would never happen.

I became uneasy about hiding the situation from Jane. Michele had stopped speaking up in class. She wouldn't go outside with me at lunchtime. If I stayed inside with her she wouldn't talk. She did nothing but draw. Or stare at the floor. Sometimes she stayed home from school, pretending to be sick, not that it was much of a pretense.

I thought Jane should know. Sitting at their kitchen table on Saturday while Jane made us cheese and onion sandwiches, I blurted it out. Michele gave me a furious look, then put her head down on the table and cried. Her hair flopped over the plate of sandwiches and I pushed it away. Jane, stricken, held her. Michele pulled off her glasses and hid her face in the crook of her mother's shoulder. She kept sobbing while Jane murmured comfort.

After a while Michele lifted her head. She rubbed wearily at her eyes and put her glasses back on. "Mum. You can't say anything! Please!"

"Why the hell not, Michele?" said Jane, straightening up. She blew her nose. "Why should this little shit get away with it? He has to stop. He has to be punished."

"You don't understand, Mum. Everybody likes him. They won't believe it. And it's so embarrassing, what they say about me." Her eyes welled up again. She covered her face with her hands.

Jane strode up and down the kitchen rubbing her hair wildly, then came back to the table. "Well, what do you want me to do, then?"

Michele looked wretched. "I don't know. Nothing."

Jane and I both did our best to help Michele over the next few weeks. Jane let her stay home as much as she wanted to. I tried to make sure that she was never by herself at school, if I could help it. I told my parents what was going on, too. At first they could hardly believe it. They thought that kind of thing had stopped since we left primary school. Best, they said, to wait it out—it would be even more horrible for Michele if the whole thing became public.

Jane insisted on talking to the headmaster, in spite of Michele's wishes. Mr. Shawcroft said he was sorry, it sounded difficult, but there was nothing he could do unless the culprits confessed or were seen in action. He found it hard to believe that Adam was behind it all. "Perhaps your daughter is mistaken about who's responsible," he said.

Jane and I kept assuring Michele that the boys would get tired of it. And in the end, probably, they would have. But meanwhile it got worse, not better. A new, disgusting rumor started going around. Adam told other kids—boys and girls—that he'd been shagging Michele since she was twelve, that she was willing and grateful because she was so ugly. How do you fight a rumor like that? I could see Michele shriveling in front of me. Something awful was happening to her, almost as though she was beginning to believe that she was this slutty person that Adam had invented for his own amusement. Almost as though she didn't care about the real Michele.

A few girls stood up for her and told her they knew it was

not true and Adam was a pig. That helped a little. But not enough.

With desperate bravado, Michele drew a savage cartoon showing a naked figure with Adam's face, caricatured but recognizable, and his trademark thick hair. He had a coiled snake in his chest in place of a heart, and another snake between his legs like a long, grotesque penis. All around the edge of the drawing fingers pointed at him.

She showed it to me, giggling a little. "I'm going to pin it up in the corridor," she said. She seemed enlivened again, more like her old self.

But I was afraid of what Adam might do to her in revenge. "Michele—I don't think you should. He'd know immediately that it was you."

She looked at me expressionlessly and closed her sketchbook.

And after that—I realized later, looking back, hating myself—Michele withdrew further and further into herself, as though there was nothing left for her to do. Every day I asked her how she was doing. Every day she would say, "I'm all right." But I knew she wasn't all right.

She went home after school one day and swallowed a bottleful of the pain pills that Dr. Barrow had prescribed for the times when the pain in her limbs was more than she could bear. Jane found her unconscious in her room and called the ambulance. But they could not save her.

Jane phoned that night from the hospital. My parents picked her up and brought her to our house. She looked like an old woman, stooped and slow with shock. My mother sat on the couch with her arms around her. We all cried. My mind went around and around all the things we could have done to help her. I couldn't believe she wasn't alive any more, that I'd never see her again. Gillian watched solemnly, coming over to us one by one to hug our knees.

Jane and my parents went to speak to Mr. Shawcroft as soon as school opened the next morning. He said he was appalled. He expressed sympathy. He said he would speak about it in the strongest possible terms to the whole school, and he would make the perpetrators so sorry and so scared that they'd never treat anyone like this again. But he couldn't talk to Adam directly, nor approach his parents. There's just no proof, he said. Only hearsay. It would lead only to more trouble, and possibly legal action against the school by Adam's family. My father argued. So did my mother. Jane didn't even try.

"I'm so sorry," said Mr. Shawcroft. "I can imagine how you feel. You have my very deepest condolences, Mrs. Ferguson."

They told me about this conversation when they got home midmorning. I hadn't gone to school. For me it was the end. I could not bear to be anywhere near Adam ever again. I wanted to go far away from the school, far away from Westerford. And that's how I ended up at Nails.

CHAPTER EIGHT

August 30, 1997, early evening

He is eager to show her his apartment, twenty minutes away. She is reluctant to leave the relative safety of the hotel. "Please, darling," he begs. "We can ignore those wolves. They'll hardly notice that we're leaving." She knows better. They notice everything. But she gives in.

The bodyguards escort them to a side door, but they are spotted as they get into the car. The reporters gun their motorbikes and swerve to follow the black Mercedes like a swarm of noxious insects. Everywhere she goes they are there, taunting and tormenting her. In the very beginning there were no photographers at all—no one knew, no one must know. The secrecy itself was bewitching. She could hardly believe it—she, of all girls, singled out for attention by the worldly prince; she, eighteen years old, shy and too tall, teased by her friends and her poised older sisters, spirited away under cover of dark to have dinner with him, alone. He seemed charmed by her awkwardness, her nervous giggles. He told her she was very pretty indeed. In his gentlemanly way he did not try to touch her. She approved. The magazines she liked to read emphasized the decorum of courting behavior. So did her favorite romantic novels where the lovers reined in their desire until all obstacles were overcome and passion swept them away.

After their first flirtatious conversation she lay in her bed spinning in giddy joy, seeing herself as he saw her—the youngest and most beautiful of the three sisters. Like a fairytale, and she the heroine, innocent, lovely, deserving. She spent hours constructing an elaborate dream of her future, when she would be a princess, proud and protected at the side of her prince. The whole world would see her as he did. "I am in love!" she repeated to herself. "I am madly in love!" She was bursting to tell all her friends but it was essential, he told her, that they be utterly discreet for the time being. It made her love burn all the hotter.

And I really was in love, she thinks, but not with him, I was in love with a fantasy, a dream of myself. When the press finally pounced on her she was at first embarrassed, then flattered by their voracious attention. It told her who she now was. It amplified her glory. The cameras were like Snow White's magic mirror, telling her over and over again that she was the fairest of all. She loved it. She enjoyed the flirtatious game of it and gave them what they wanted—the dazzling smile, the demure glance over a bare shoulder. Until they got annoying, and refused to leave her alone when she begged them. And then they became cruel, some of them, shouting obscene insults to make her break down and cry in mortification and try to run away. Then they would grin in triumph as they snapped the pictures of a disheveled, wretched princess that would put fat wads of money in their pockets. They're like bloodhounds, she thinks, frenzied with the chase. They won't rest until they've torn me to pieces.

She despises them but even now she invites their attentions. She can't help it, and hates herself for doing it. She visited a battered women's shelter once, hugging children who'd been forced to leave their homes, talking to women for whom the hopefulness of love had turned into a nightmare of abuse and humiliation. They talked about their husbands and boyfriends, how they kept forgiving them and loving them in spite of everything, until finally they realized they were in danger, their children as well. She'd listened with her usual compassion. Inside she was saying—but I'm like you! Not with a husband but with those men with their cameras who claim to love me, who abuse me and harass me wherever I go. She was ashamed to admit how much she still needed them, in spite of hating them. I need courage like you, she thought, but did not say aloud to the women, courage to turn my back on them once and for all.

She remembers being eight years old, playing in the sunny nursery with her little brother. A fly landed on her bare leg and instead of brushing it away she let it crawl up and down. The light tickling was pleasurable, like being stroked with a tiny feather. Her brother noticed and stuck out his own stubby legs until a fly landed on him too. Then another. They watched the flies crawling on their skin, faintly guilty at this unexpected pleasure. Then they got tired of it. They shooed the flies away and killed them one by one with a rolled-up comic book.

Careening through the city streets, she suppresses a hiccup of laughter. That's what she needs now. A giant rolled-up comic book to squash those pests flat to the ground, their poisonous juices leaking. Her lover, ever vigilant, catches her moment of mirth and laughs with her, though he has no idea what has amused her. Poor man, she thinks. It's not his fault that he bores me rigid. He's given me all he's capable of giving. She thinks with a spike of guilt about her contempt for his lack of knowledge or curiosity about anything beyond his privileged existence. She knows what it feels like to be despised. She lets her hand lie in his and nestles into his warm shoulder. He tightens his arm around her.

CHAPTER NINE

Alex

I was sitting in the living room reading when they showed the first interview with Prince Charles and his fiancée. When I glanced up at the television I noticed a girl in a blue outfit standing beside the prince, who seemed very chuffed. The girl seemed too young for him.

At first she didn't look familiar at all. Then she did.

"Nah," I said aloud. "Couldn't be." I looked more carefully. It was her. It was my Diana. I stopped listening to what the prince was saying. My Diana was standing in front of a mass of cameras with the Prince of Wales. It was the most bizarre thing, like seeing Snow White or Cinderella alive and speaking on television. I knew Diana was a real person, of course. We'd talked to each other, sort of. We'd danced together. I'd touched her hands. But for four years she'd been my secret treasure, known only to me. She had become like a fictional person as far as I was concerned. I knew absolutely nothing about her real life. I didn't know her last name. It wasn't that I was in love with her—I wasn't that daft. She was just my Diana. "My" is a funny word. It means possession, but who is the possessor? My book. My friend. My family. My town. In this case, to call her "my" Diana meant, and still means, something particular. It's as though she was a star that shone for me alone. Or a hidden part of my body, like a vital organ inside me.

I had no illusion that I meant anything whatsoever to her. I was not "her" Alex. She'd never remember me, ever.

But here she was. Not imaginary. All these years, while I'd been at Nails, and then back at home doing nothing and getting depressed, then finally becoming a student, Diana had been somewhere too. She'd had an actual existence, during which she'd met Prince Charles and got to know him and agreed to marry him.

I stared at them on the screen, his plain face and cultured voice, her eyes almost hidden by her hair, the engagement ring held out to catch the light as the cameras flashed.

I, crippled Alex from Westerford, North Devon, knew a girl who was a Lady and was going to be a princess. A future queen. I had danced with her. We had laughed together. I had thought of her every day for four years.

I had to tell someone.

Fortunately for me, no one was home. By the time my mother came back I'd realized what a great mistake it would be to tell her, or anyone. Just imagining the conversation was mortifying enough:

"Mum! Wait till I tell you!"

"Tell me what?"

"That girl who's just got engaged to Charles? Well—I met her, at Nails! She danced with me!"

At this point, my mother would look at me with sympathy and a touch of amusement. "Did she, now?" And I would be forced to imagine the scene from her point of view, her drooling boy in his wheelchair, the aristocratic visitor taking a kind but momentary interest in him, then poor deluded Alex obsessing about it for years.

I could not bear to think about it like that. So I said nothing until I was calm enough to be careful. I waited until the dinner table conversation went to the royal news.

"I think that girl came to Nails once," I said. "With her school." My parents were mildly interested. Gillian was gratifyingly impressed. "Did she really, Alex? What was she wearing?"

"Her school uniform, silly," said my mother.

I said nothing about our dance. None of them suspected who Diana really was for me.

Within twenty-four hours it seemed as though the entire population of Great Britain fell in love with Lady Diana. The entire population of the world. I could hardly think of her as mine anymore. I found it hard to get used to, though I took pleasure in being able to say her name out loud, at last. Her photo was in the paper every day, her life story was written up in endless detail, there were interviews with her friends, her nannies, anyone who'd ever known her. Except me. They didn't ask me. I felt like I knew her in a way that no one else did. Who else had danced with her in a wheelchair? Who else had recognized how extraordinary she was when she was only fifteen? No one, that's who. Only me.

Even in a household like ours, where royalty inspired jokes rather than reverence, we all became experts on her life. We learned about her sisters and younger brother, her scandalously divorced parents, the family mansion, her inadequate education, her fondness for children, and so on. We learned that she did not like polo. All kinds of useless information.

None of it explained what made people love her. What it was about her that had made me think about her every day of my life after meeting her for five minutes and exchanging exactly two words with her. I tried hard to figure it out. It wasn't just that she was beautiful. It wasn't just that she was going to be a princess, and then a queen, which of course was something that neither she nor I knew when I met her. No. There was something about her. That's all you could say. An unusual kind of adorableness, along with a sort of light that shone from her towards other people. It was as though each person that she met, shook hands with, laughed with—each of those people felt themselves seen for a moment, and loved. It seemed ridiculously corny to say it. But that's what it was like.

Whatever it was, I'd felt it, and now everyone and his auntie felt it too. Everyone except, as we all found out eventually, the prince and his family, who were quite immune to her magic.

The royal romance dominated not only the media but every casual conversation—the milkman wanted to talk about it, the bus driver, Sandra, the waitress in the only café in Westerford where I could get in with my wheelchair. "Her big sister thought she was going to be the one!" Sandra said, putting our fish and chips down in front of us. "Not very happy about it, so I heard."

I was in a dilemma. I badly wanted to watch Diana's wedding on television. I wanted to see her in her peak of glory. But no one else in my family would be watching. If I told them that I wanted to, they'd tease me forever. My parents thought the whole business was an overblown display masking very pragmatic calculations. "It's all about reproduction," said my father, watching a cluster of television personalities salivate about the couple's plans for children. "She was probably shortlisted as a potential breeder when she was five years old. Titled family, nice-looking, not too bright. And not Catholic. All she had to do was keep her virginity."

"Dad," I said, "that is disgusting. They love each other. You can see it." I didn't want to think about the cold demands of the monarchy.

He was amused. "Didn't know you were such a romantic, Alex." He rumpled my hair, which annoyed me. "Don't worry, old boy, I'm sure they'll live happily ever after."

My mother felt sorry for Diana. She and the rest of my family had adopted the way I said her name, the way I'd heard her say it. "A sacrificial lamb, poor child," my mother said, shaking her head over a Sunday supplement cover where Diana, who'd become slender and stylish and ravishingly pretty, beamed like a little girl who'd won a prize. It looked to me like she was having a great time being the princess-to-be, madly adored by so many people, photographed dozens of times a day in one fancy outfit after another. I thought she was having fun with it all, a teenager suddenly learning how beautiful and glamorous she could be. We didn't know about the other side of it.

Clearly my parents were not going to watch the wedding of the century, as the media were calling it. Gillian unwittingly came to my rescue. Independent-minded though they were, she and her best friend Polly had decided that they, too, adored Diana. "We don't like him," Gillian explained. "But we love her." They begged my parents to let them commandeer the living room for the entire day of the wedding so they could watch without interruption.

"It's not fair to Alex," objected my mother. "What's he supposed to do while you're wallowing in all that pomp and circumstance?" She and my father could sit upstairs, or go out, but I usually sat in my corner of the room, reading or writing.

"I don't mind," I said. "Maybe I'll watch it with you." Having your facial features in motion all the time comes in handy sometimes. It was easy for me to hide my desperate eagerness. Gillian jumped up and hugged me. "Oh thank you, thank you, thank you!"

She and Polly dressed up like brides for the occasion, using petticoats and lace curtains. They picked bunches of flowers. They wanted to borrow a top hat for me but I refused. My mother indulged us by making a wedding feast with cucumber sandwiches and chocolate cake. She put out the champagne glasses that she had bought for their twentieth anniversary, with a jug of orange juice.

We started watching right after breakfast. I sat impatiently through the boring footage of two million eager people crowding along the route from Clarence House to St Paul's Cathedral with their flowers and flags. Assorted celebrities speculated excitedly about her wedding dress and how she might wear her blonde hair.

And then, finally, there she was, as beautiful as a princess bride could possibly be. Gillian and Polly were so busy screaming that they did not see that I had to dab my leaking eyes, to my embarrassment. Diana leaned forward in the glass carriage, beside her stunned-looking father, and waved to all the people who adored her. I hoped vehemently that her life would be everything that she wanted.

I wished that Michele was there to watch the wedding with us. She would have had funny things to say about the guests in their absurd hats, and Prince Charles looking so stiff. I looked at them all with her eyes, now and then, and saw what a stuffy lot of people they seemed. Michele would have liked Diana, I thought. Diana wasn't remote and formal like the rest of the royal family. She was someone we could have talked to, Michele and I.

While I was at Nails, Jane had moved to a little river town a few miles the other side of Westerford. We got together now and then. Sometimes we talked about what Michele would be doing if she hadn't died. It was comforting to give her this imaginary life. We were sure she'd have boyfriends and eventually get married. She'd find someone decent, someone we liked. They'd have children. And she'd have an interesting job as well. I watched a story on television about a disabled travel agent who specialized in sending people off to places like Samarkand or Patagonia. "One day I'm going to jolly well get on the plane and see for myself!" the woman had said, smiling from her wheelchair. I could see Michele doing something like that. Or perhaps she'd be a successful artist. She wouldn't live in Westerford. She'd have found a place where the misery of her school days was not embedded in the streets and buildings and the faces of people who had let her suffer. She'd come and see us when she could.

Diana got pregnant immediately, to smug approval from Buckingham Palace and wild jubilation from everyone else. I couldn't help recalling my father's cynical comments about breeding. On Midsummer's Day, less than a year after the wedding, her son was born. It was as though Jesus Christ himself had been born again, here in England. I was happy for Diana. I thought she'd be a very good mother even though she was still so young. She'd already had so much practice looking after small children. In the photos she looked tender and entranced, holding her baby in his lacy shawls. But I also felt uneasy. She seemed so subdued, overwhelmed by everything around her, the press hovering, the hungry attention of millions of strangers. Everyone seemed to own this baby. What must it feel like to hold your infant and know that he was going to be a king some day?

Diana seemed a diminished figure. She smiled out of every front page. We never heard her voice.

CHAPTER TEN

August 30, 1997, evening

The sky has darkened and rain is falling. The apartment is opulent but unwelcoming, the air lifeless, as though the windows have not been opened for months. He pours cognac for them both. Soon they'll go to a nightclub, then dinner—the most glamorous nightclub, the most fashionable restaurant. It cheers her to think of the sophisticated and lovely people who'll be at the club, the excited chatter in several languages and the pulsing music. Perhaps she'll dance. She loves to dance. She considers her dresses, already pressed and hung in the guest dressing room by discreet hands. She puts on a sleek black gown with one bare shoulder. Her hair is perfect. "You are a goddess," her lover whispers in her ear, standing behind her as she looks in the mirror. Her skin is immaculately smooth and tan from weeks on the Mediterranean and the pampering of rare botanicals. I do look good, she thinks. I look strong. She remembers her most damaged self, two years before, when she exposed herself so horribly in that BBC interview. She is proud now of her health and strength. I am ready for anything, she thinks. I am ready to take my place.

He encircles her from behind and presses his face to her neck. She watches their entwined image in the mirror, the slim blue-eyed woman, the dark-haired man ecstatic with her scent and her sculpted body. He slips the single black strap off her shoulder and slides the zipper down. The mirror shows his curly head, his restless hands. His breath in the crook of her neck sends fire along her nerves. She melts back into his body and lets the dress fall to the floor. She turns to him, eyes closed now, passive in his arms. He backs out of the upholstered dressing room and over to his bed, half carrying her. He unfastens his own clothes. His body is taut, the skin warm and smooth. She surrenders to him. He devours her. Her body's pleasure effaces the world beyond this semi-dark room and the wide disheveled bed. "The driver..." she murmurs, remembering their plans. "He'll wait," he says. Of course he'll wait.

They lie facing each other, bodies satiated. She stares into his eyes. She sees nothing, a blank brown gaze without depth. For a moment she is terrified, as though she'd looked into a mirror and seen no reflection. She rolls onto her side, away from him. He strokes her back, mews of remembered pleasure in his throat.

She thinks of a flat she once visited, the home of a friend's mother, an artist—an unlikely mother for her un-bohemian friend who was clambering up the ladder of Tory politics. The flat was on the upper two floors of a graceful house opposite a small park. The windows were tall, uncurtained, open to the sky and the nearby roofs and treetops. A cheerful, bustling London stretched into the distance. Down on the street a young man rode past on a bicycle leading seven dogs of assorted sizes, the littlest ones racing on their short legs to keep up. It made her laugh. The artist's paintings were everywhere, framed and unframed, covering the walls, stacked against chairs, sketches covering the dining table. She thought they were brilliant. The woman had painted what she saw out her windows, as well as vibrant bunches of flowers and people looking humorously or earnestly at the viewer. Inside the fireplace, neatly stacked, was a child's dream collection of miniature cars, puppets, dolls, and dolls' furniture, ready for visits from the artist's grandchildren. The woman herself was friendly but distant, as though she would like to get back to the painting on her easel.

I wish I could live in a flat like that, she thinks now. And be an ordinary person, an ordinary mother. Looking after my boys with no one watching over my shoulder.

And why couldn't I? Why not? She projects herself into the artist's flat and feels an immediate and vivid sense of freedom. Just her and her sons, when they weren't at school. She'd have a little office on the top floor, with a lovely view. A secretary would come in each day to help her with her visits and her travel. If her new bold idea comes to fruition she'll have a more public office somewhere else, of course. They'd make sure she had a car, and a driver. I must try Hugh again, she thinks. She'll have to sneak out to the phone in the entranceway.

The artist had had a pot of soup simmering on her stove when they visited. Her friend helped himself to a bowl of it as though it was his kitchen, his soup, and his mother teased him. She can't remember if she ever made soup herself, in her cooking days. She used to be quite good at roast lamb, and cakes. Perhaps she'll take a cooking class, why not? Learn some new tricks. Cook for the boys. She sees herself tying on a striped apron, surveying her copper-bottomed pots and pans, composing a satisfying meal.

She'd need new friends for this new life. She's tired of the jaded acquaintances who only want to talk about who's bonking who, who's getting married and divorced, and how expensively, what the coolest restaurant is these days and what they are serving. They don't cook for themselves, these people. No, she'll need new friends who are not aristocratic or rich, certainly not royal. People who live in flats or terrace houses and look after their own children and do work that's clearly useful. She's met thousands of people like that, of course, but she hasn't got to know them. Not yet.

Her lover has dozed off, snoring lightly into her back, leaving her free to devise her new existence.

She sees herself in jeans, not the designer dresses that stuff her wardrobe now and fill multiple suitcases when she travels. Jeans and a casual shirt. That's what she prefers, anyway.

But a sneering voice breaks into her thoughts. "Idiot! You really think you're going to give up your tiaras and your Catherine Walkers? Give up all this attention? Come on! Don't fool yourself!"

She knows it's come to this. She's going to have to choose. A life of helping others, and going home to her nice, comfortable flat and her sons. Or this life, decorated with diamonds, gratifying the greedy press, wasting her time in the dull company of a bored and boring playboy.

She eases out of the playboy's sleeping arms. Somewhere in this apartment there must be the makings of a cup of tea. She picks up his shirt off the floor and slips it on, then goes into the lavish, unused kitchen. She finds an electric kettle, a cup, a single box of teabags. She pours boiling water. The scent of Earl Grey heartens her. She is pleased with herself for making her own tea. I can do it, she tells the sneering voice. Don't you tell me I can't do it. She disposes of the teabag and looks for the phone.

CHAPTER ELEVEN

Alex

When I was at Nails, doing well in my classes, playing our non-standard versions of cricket and tennis, writing witty scripts for the drama club, I fully expected to go on to university. I fancied myself like all those undergrads in the books and films. I'd go to tutorials with dons in academic gowns. I'd sit by a slow-moving river reading a weighty novel while friends punted by and waved. I'd let my hair grow longer, I'd meet interesting people, perhaps including girls. I even had a fantasy about crossing paths with Diana. I pictured us strolling across a quad together—her strolling, me wheeling; the two of us in a class together, me surprising her with my confidence and knowledge. I thought I might be one of those very clever chaps who wrote hilarious skits, like the Pythons, even if I couldn't act in it. In my boldest dreams I became famous, proving to the cruel kids at school that they were wrong to treat me so badly.

When I talked to the headmaster about university he just sighed. "Alex. I don't think it's on the cards." He paused. I knew he was looking for words that would hurt as little as possible. "Universities aren't set up for chaps like you, unfortunately. Even the newer ones." He talked about steps and stairs, and buildings with narrow doors, and old-fashioned lavatories. I got the idea. He didn't even have to mention my hesitant speech—better than it was, but strangers still strained to understand me—and my dependence on typewriters. You can't take lecture notes on a typewriter.

I honestly hadn't let myself think about those kinds of obstacles. But it was perfectly obvious, now that he pointed them out. How could I have thought for a second that I could fit in?

"I do think it'll be different one day," Mr. Donahue said. "A lot of people think it isn't fair, the way things are at present. But for now..." He didn't have to go on.

So I finished school and went home, with my A-levels that were about as much use as last year's wall calendar from the petrol station.

My parents were happy to have me home again, and Gillian, in her eight-year old way, was thrilled. But it was different from coming home for the summer holidays. I wasn't leaving. I was a fixture. If I didn't find something to do with myself I was going to sit in my parents' living room like a sack of onions for the rest of our lives.

For a while I structured my days around wheeling down to the river to watch the birds and the tide. Sometimes I'd stop on the bridge, thinking about the Romans who built it a thousand years ago. I liked seeing the tide filling up the riverbed like a drink of water for a thirsty person. Each day the curving line of water and sand was a little different. I tried to memorize it from one day to the next, wishing I could paint it as Michele would have been able to. I missed her sharply. Coming back to

Westerford would have been very different if she'd been there. My father gave me a camera, adapted for people with twisted hands, and I tried to record the changing face of the river. But what I saw with my eye became flat and dull in the prints.

The days started drawing in and the wind took on an icy edge. I'd been getting up late so as not to be in the way while my family rushed up and down the stairs, boiled the kettle, banged the front door. Now, with the cold rain beating against my window, I didn't want to get up at all—haul my body out of bed, get myself to the bathroom under the stairs, deal with my cumbersome ablutions, go back and drag my clothes on. Find something to eat in the kitchen.

It didn't seem worth it.

I read about a man who lost his sense of smell and taste after an accident. He ate in order to live, but he found it disgusting to have food in his mouth that had texture but no flavor. My life no longer had any flavor. Even the thought of Diana didn't help. The memory of our dance had withered, like an old bunch of flowers. The only thing that got my blood going was hearing one day that Adam Widmer had joined the army and was in officers' training at Sandhurst. Jane had cut out a little newspaper article, complete with flattering photo. "Daddy must have pulled some strings," she said. I looked at the photo with disgust. I hoped Adam would be posted to some unpleasant, dangerous place and get captured by a merciless enemy. But most of all, I wanted his own cruelty exposed and punished. I was sure he was still making other people wretched.

Once that little flurry of rage subsided I was as lifeless as before. A book in the school library said that bodies like mine are tough on organs and bones. People like me often don't live past middle age. Our systems wear out early. I would never kill myself. But I thought maybe nature would take care of it. I could just wait for my systems to wear out. If the old almshouses near the Strand hadn't been turned into posh flats, they could just stow me away there, I thought, along with all the other human mistakes. I'd always avoided passing the almshouses if I could, with their grim dark porches. Now I lingered, imagining.

My parents and Gillian seemed to come from some alien planet where everyone buzzed around with not a doubt in their minds about their tasks and destinations. I didn't want my morbid thoughts to disturb them. So I forced myself to get up before they came home, planting myself in the corner with a book on my lap as though I'd had a nice day reading.

My mother sat down beside me one day and took the book, which was upside down, out of my hands. "It's hard. I know," she said. "I wish we weren't all so busy."

I tried to stir myself. "I'm glad you're busy."

"Yes, but…Alex, don't you want to be doing something yourself?"

Of course I wanted to be doing something. It was just that there was nothing I could do. I couldn't get a job. I couldn't go to university. I still felt crushed by that disappointment, as though all the universities in Britain had stood together with their arms folded and said, "You, Alex Carr, don't belong with us, because you're a cripple." If I were a braver person I could tell them to fuck off, I can read and study and write without you. But I wasn't that brave person.

"Yes, Mum," was all I said. "Such as."

"I want you to think about the Open University again."

She'd tried to persuade me before. I wasn't interested in distance learning. If I couldn't go to an ordinary university I didn't want to go at all.

"Please, Alex. It worked out so well for me." She'd finished her degree, finally, while I was at boarding school, and then trained as a social worker. It was perfect for her. She'd never been so contented.

I shook my head.

She left a prospectus and an application form on my desk, just in case. The next day I looked at them. They had hundreds of courses. And they encouraged applications from disabled people. If I applied, and they turned me down, I'd be no worse off than I already was. I filled out the form.

When Gillian announced that Diana was coming to Westerford I didn't believe it.

"No, she really is, Alex. Look at this!" She waved the newspaper in front of me. We were having breakfast before she went off to school. My parents had already left for work. I looked at the front page that Gillian thrust at me. "PRINCESS TO VISIT NORTH DEVON." Three years after the wedding she was still big news. She was pregnant again, expecting in September. The article said that she'd be in Westerford for a morning and would do a walkabout along the Strand before opening a new radiology unit at the hospital. Just her, not Charles. It was clear by then that the crowds were much more interested in her than him and she often made official visits by herself. My heart squeezed and my breath felt short. Diana was still my secret treasure. I couldn't not go and see her if she was nearby. But to be one of hundreds of pathetically besotted punters ogling her from the side of the road—and me more pathetic than all of them—that also seemed impossible.

"Let's go!" said Gillian. It was so simple for her.

I hesitated. She misunderstood my reluctance. "Please, Alex!

Please come with me! I don't want go by myself." Gillian was completely skeptical about the monarchy but Diana was another matter altogether. "I need moral support!"

"OK," I said. "I'll go with you." I didn't tell her that I'd need moral support a lot more than she would. Gillian would provide it without even trying.

The visit was two weeks away. The small part of my being that was always focused on Diana threatened to erupt out of control.

It would be the first time since Nails that I was in the same physical space as her—that I would see her, hear her, breath the same air as her. The question that burnt into me like a torturer's wire was, would she see me? Would she pause in front of me, just by chance? And if her gaze fell on me, what would she see? A skinny, feeble person in a wheelchair? Would my face seem familiar? Would she remember being fifteen years old and dancing with a crippled boy at his school?

I knew she would not. But I could not stop myself from imagining what could happen, what was technically not beyond the realm of possibility: Diana pauses in front of me and Gillian, accepts Gillian's flowers with a smile, then looks at me, looks again, says—"Oh—I think we've met" and I say, "Yes, your Highness, years ago you visited my school, and we danced together" and the words would come out clearly so she could understand, and she would reach out her gloved hand for me to shake, and the cameras would flash, and she would say, "Yes, of course, I remember! Please tell me your name again," and I would tell her, and she would say "Alex, it's lovely to see you again. Do take good care of yourself," and I would smile and let her go, aloft with joy.

"Give it up," I said to myself in disgust when this moronic

fantasy refused to die a decent death. But I couldn't give it up. I resigned myself to living in dreamland until the day came and went and I could awaken.

"You're what?" said my mother when Gillian and I appeared in the kitchen on the morning of the walkabout. "Dear oh dear. Well, off you go, my poor little royalists. Give my regards to HRH."

It was a nice enough early summer day, cool but sunny with fast-moving clouds blowing in from the Irish Sea. The tide was full. We set off over the bridge early so that we'd be ensconced in a good spot before the crowds came. Forcing a wheelchair through a crush of ardent loyal subjects would not be fun. We found a place right in front of the Albert clock where no one would block our view of Diana. Or hers of me. We waited. The excited chatter around us made it hard to talk, which was a relief. My heart thumped erratically like a confused mallet in my chest. I was wearing sunglasses, which helped. I'd worn a nice shirt and trousers, too, camouflaged by my ordinary jacket to deflect more teasing, though if I'd had a nicer jacket I would have worn it.

From further up the Strand the noise of the crowd swelled. "She's here! She's here!" people around us began to shout. Her entourage came into view: a row of solemn-looking policemen, their suspicious gazes swiveling from side to side. Then a cluster of important people from the mayor's office. I recognized a couple of them, large ladies done up in their Sunday best. Well, I couldn't blame them. They'd talk about this day for the rest of their lives.

And then there she was. Walking along beside the mayor and his wife. Wearing a pink outfit and carrying pink and yellow flowers. She looked tall and slender, barely pregnant. No hat. Her hair longer and blonder than I remembered it. She seemed so familiar, from all the thousands of photos and television appearances I'd seen. She walked slowly, approaching one side of the street and then the other, reaching out to touch the outstretched hands, to take up a posy of flowers and sniff it appreciatively, then hand it to one of the women walking behind her. There was nothing false or reserved in her manner. You'd swear she was happy to be there. "Isn't she lovely," people breathed all around us. "Isn't she beautiful. Our princess."

And that quality she had, that I'd felt when we were fifteen, that shone out of every photo—it was there, palpable, right there in our little square, amplified and reflected back to her by the people lining the street.

She drew closer to where Gillian and I waited. I think my heart actually stopped for a few beats. I could have died right there in front of her. She bent down to whisper to a little girl standing to our left, then straightened and moved on past us, pausing again to shake hands with an old codger with his war medals on.

She didn't look at me.

Behind me, Gillian squeezed my shoulder. I twisted my neck to look up at her, grateful for my sunglasses. Gillian understood. I could see it in her face. She couldn't know about my meeting with Diana, because I'd never told anyone. But she understood anyway. I managed a weak smile and turned back. Diana was still just a few feet beyond us, smiling, greeting, embracing all of us in her kind blue gaze.

Close behind her and the mayoral party was her military escort, six handsome young soldiers, sauntering casually. One of them caught my attention. Loathing flooded me even before I actually recognized him. And then I realized that others were recognizing him too—the Westerford boy home in triumph. "Adam!" they shouted. "Lieutenant Widmer!" He grinned, enjoying the glory.

Hearing the shouts, Diana turned back toward him and paused so he could catch up with her. She put her hand on his arm and said something, laughing. Tall as she was, he was taller. He leant down to her, nodding with a charming smile. She continued the walkabout. Adam fell back into line with the other soldiers.

She had distracted him at the right moment so he didn't see me, thank goodness. I don't know if I could have endured meeting his eyes and seeing either his recognition of me, or the lack of it. I would have needed to kill him.

I was feeling very ill. I did not want to have a seizure out here on the street. "Gillian?" I said, reaching for her arm.

"Shall we try and get out of here?" she said. "I'm ready."

I was sick for a couple of weeks after Diana's walkabout. My neurology couldn't take it. The excruciating excitement of seeing her after all those years. And then Adam Widmer in her entourage. Not the figure of shame that I had invented in my revenge fantasies but admired by everyone—admired by her! They knew and liked each other. I saw her touch him. My Diana's hand on the arm of the person I detested most in the world. There wasn't any place inside me that this image could live peacefully. It eroded the small strength that I had in my bones and muscles and I couldn't hold myself upright at all.

I hated being even more of a trouble to my family than I was already. For a few days I had to lie in my room and let others do everything for me. I tried to insist that I'd be all right when my parents were at work and Gillian at school, but they got a nurse in anyway. She was young-ish, no sense of humor, large and strong as she had to be in her line of work. She was all right. She did what she needed to do, and left me alone the rest of the time. I could hear the television going nonstop in the living room. I didn't care.

Gillian came straight to my room as soon as she got home from school each day, trying to cheer me up. Poor girl. Here she was, thirteen years old, pretty and bright, in mind and body as able as they come, tethered to a helpless heap like me. Tethered by love. Not much you can do about that.

She knew that something had happened for me out there on the square, but she knew better than to ask me about it. She tried all kinds of things to divert me, most of all Diana stories, of which there was no shortage. The press was getting louder and louder on the subject of Diana's supposed unhappiness. It still seemed like nasty gossip to me. She was the mother of a sweet little boy, about to have another baby. She was more beautiful than ever, still beloved by millions of people everywhere in the world. How could she be the neurotic person they were now describing, someone who had tantrums and an eating disorder? I'd never even heard of eating disorders. When I learned what bulimia was I could not associate something so absurd and ugly with Diana. It was very strange, I thought, how the newspapers and television journalists could fawn on her and adore her and at the same time publish such cruel things about her. I tried to think what it must be like for her. It reminded me of Michele, defenseless in the face of rumors and insults. Did Diana try to ignore all those stories? Did she want to stand up and scream, "Leave me alone! You've got it all wrong!" Did she weep in vexation? And the prince—was he kind? Did he put his arms around her and comfort her? Or did he blame her for all the attention?

"Oh my goodness," said Gillian. She was sitting on my bed with the Guardian.

"What?" I said. I didn't have the energy to turn my head.

"Don't know if you want to hear this."

"I don't care."

"All right, then, I'll tell you. They're talking about Charles meeting up with this horsy-faced old tart he used to get around with. I don't believe it. Diana's about ten million times prettier than her."

I looked at the photo of the prince and the woman beside him at a polo match. They looked like friends, not lovers. The woman was blowzy and plain. "Doesn't mean a thing. Diana doesn't like polo, that's all."

It was inconceivable that a man with the extraordinary good luck to be married to Diana would ever look another woman. If anyone had reason to be unsatisfied in that marriage, it was Diana, surely, with an older, rather staid and unattractive husband. But she wouldn't betray him. She had made her vows. So had he. They loved each other. They had a family. I dismissed the Guardian story, cross with them for indulging in gossip like a tabloid.

CHAPTER TWELVE

August 30, 1997, evening.

She tiptoes to the entranceway where a portable phone lies on a hall table. She tries Hugh and waits again for the annoying message to finish. "Phone me back," she says softly. "I'll be here a while longer." She gives him the number that she sees on the phone. There is no need to identify herself. Hugh has known her voice since they flirted for a while at the age of seventeen, before he told her regretfully that he really preferred men.

Her lover is still sleeping. She wants more than anything to go for a walk, to stroll alone in the gathering darkness, wandering the nearby streets, perhaps finding a park or a square where she could sit and watch people enjoying the last evening of the summer before August is over and Paris returns to its busy self. But she cannot. It is not possible for her to go for a walk like any other person might. Her freedom has been confiscated. A life sentence without parole. Unless she releases herself, if she has the courage, and a large dollop of luck.

Could she escape in disguise? She looks down at the shirt she is wearing, her lover's white silk shirt. A mischievous thought seizes her. She finds his trousers where he dropped them on the floor and pulls them on. The length is right but they are much too large in the waist. She looks around and finds a small pillow, stuffs it inside the pants and shirt and buckles the belt so it will stay put. She looks in a mirror and nearly giggles out loud, then claps her hand to her mouth. She doesn't want to wake him.

Her blond head contradicts the portly body in the mirror. Quietly, she opens drawers and closet doors. They're mostly empty. He doesn't really live here. It's one of several perches, all of them, she imagines, sumptuous and impersonal like this. She takes a black cashmere coat off a hanger and drapes it around her shoulders. There's a cap on a shelf above, the kind of thing a middle-aged golfer might wear. She stuffs her hair into it and looks again in the mirror. Better. She feels the excitement she used to feel as a child, dressing up in clothes purloined from her father's and mother's wardrobes, turning herself into someone different. Sometimes one of her sisters or her brother would join her in the game, prancing along corridors, posing in front of tall ornate mirrors. Her mother had moved away. She lived in London in a flat and cried when they came to visit her. She wanted the children to live with her but their father said no, she wasn't a good mother. Some of her clothes remained in the bedroom that had been hers. A few dresses, a fur coat, a pink shantung suit. They smelled of her perfume and her face powder, a hint of cigarettes. Wearing them was like being enclosed again in her mother's arms, her mother's silky cheek next to hers.

She sniffs her lover's black coat. There is only the tinge of dry cleaning fluid. She takes her make-up bag into the bathroom and ponders herself in the wall-length mirror, then carefully draws a moustache and small beard with mascara and eyeliner. She puts on her sunglasses and tries different walks, swaggering, stooped, spring-heeled. "Bloody hell," she says triumphantly to her unrecognizable image. She imagines tiptoeing out, flying down the stairs to the street, and walking off in anonymous freedom. She imagines her lover's bewilderment when he wakes and she's not there. His panicked call to the bodyguards waiting outside.

It's impossible. The bodyguards would see her leave. They'd know it was her. Of course they would. They'd either follow her, a few paces behind, or they'd remonstrate with her and make her go back inside.

She tears off the borrowed clothes and runs a bath, her exhilaration vanished. The water is almost scalding. She scrubs the moustache and beard off her face and lies back in the heat and steam. How did I get myself locked up like this, she thinks. She sits up in the bath and runs cold water to splash on her face. All those people who claim to love me so much. Who don't even know me. It's they who've made me a prisoner.

She comes back to the bed. He is still sleeping, his fleshy bare shoulder twitching a little. He is dreaming. She wonders what he dreams about. She has no idea. Egypt, perhaps. White buildings in bright sunlight. People speaking Arabic. She knows nothing about Egypt. She lies down beside him, above the covers. There is nowhere else for her to go.

CHAPTER THIRTEEN

Alex

The Open University accepted me. And I liked it more than I thought I would, once I got used to the idea that I'd never meet my instructors or fellow students face to face.

The best thing about it was finding a network of disabled students like me. I had plenty of disabled friends at Nails, but these friends were different. They talked about rights. They said that ordinary people, and the government, had a responsibility to make life more manageable for people like us. It had never occurred to me. I thought it was our job to accept our weirdness and make the best of it. The disability rights people wrote letters to newspapers and members of Parliament, they got themselves on the radio and television. In London and other big cities they would sometimes gather in their wheelchairs to obstruct an inaccessible building, forcing able-bodied people to look at them and listen to them.

Nothing like that happened in Westerford. There weren't enough of us. But I became an activist in my own way, writing letters, signing petitions, voting, helping with the newsletter.

At a regional conference I found myself telling a roomful of people about Michele and Adam, how he'd driven her to suicide and got away with it. I didn't mention him and Diana, still painful in my mind like a cut that wouldn't heal. Afterwards a woman asked me if I'd speak to the children at her school, not far from Westerford. Me, a speaker, with my strange, slow, hard to understand speech! Talking to other disabled people was one thing but I wasn't sure I could talk to a group of normals—especially kids. Would they be cruel, like my own schoolmates?

But I did it. I told our story, or at least parts of it. The children listened, mouths open.

A few weeks later I was invited to another school, then another. By the time I was in my late twenties, a graduate with a degree, I had what you might call a career. At least a calling. And it even brought me a bit of money, which I casually left on the kitchen table as my contribution to household expenses. By then it was just me and my mother living at home. My father had finally packed up and left, having fulfilled his side of the bargain, which was to stick around until I either died or grew up. He wasn't far away, living with his girlfriend Jess. Gillian was at university in London, doing brilliantly.

There was one other person from Westerford in the disability rights network, a woman called Wendy. She was older than me and much more disabled. We corresponded by email a few times—email had recently entered and changed all of our lives, letting us converse easily across barriers of distance and handicaps. Wendy was in a motorized chair, she told me, and could talk only through an electronic keyboard. In emails she was as communicative as anyone else. "Come and see me, if you'd like to," she wrote, after a while.

Wendy lived in a group home called Three Wells on the outskirts of Westerford. She was a thin woman in faded blue ski trousers, her body and face skewed to one side. After we'd been talking a few minutes she wheeled away from me abruptly and I thought that she was frustrated with our conversation. But she was turning herself around so that I could read her board as she typed. She listened to me attentively, then composed a response on her keyboard, her left hand waving in the air before hitting the keys with apparent randomness, landing on exactly the one she wanted. I read her sentences aloud as they took form, or waited for the robotic voice to pronounce them when she was finished. We both knew how to be patient. That's something people like us are good at.

Wendy told me about growing up in institutions with dozens of other discarded kids. It was the fate that my father's mother would have chosen for me. Wendy hadn't seen her family since she was two years old. She'd survived thanks to an observant aide who'd recognized her intelligence and insisted that she receive tutoring. I told her about my schooling, my family. After a while I told her about Michele. Wendy closed her eyes. Her crooked mouth gaped in sorrow. She typed something on her board. "Justice will come," the electronic voice said.

Unlike Wendy, who was studying for a PhD, the other eight residents at Three Wells were mentally as well as physically handicapped. I couldn't help it, I didn't want to be near them and I especially didn't want to be seen as one of them. I'd worked so hard all my life to prove that inside my strange-looking body I was a normal person. I didn't fill my days with "activities" like the sing-alongs where the residents moaned and barked like seals while a well-meaning woman played her guitar and sang

Michael Row Your Boat Ashore. Some of the residents went off in a van each morning to assemble plastic key chains, chuffed to be going off to work like the seven dwarves.

One day when I came to visit, Wendy was getting ready to go for a walk with four of the other residents and a couple of aides. "Join us!" she gestured. I was reluctant.

"What's your name?" asked a spidery middle-aged man with sparse, carefully combed dark hair and a constant smile. I told him. "Mine's Bill," he said. "Bill," he repeated, thumping his chest. He wasn't difficult to understand but I knew he would have nothing of interest to say.

There was a bitter wind off the river. Getting everyone's hats and coats and gloves on took half an hour. We finally set off, a phalanx of six wheelchairs and two perpendicular people, heading towards the park. Wendy and I didn't talk since she couldn't respond while we were in motion. The others prattled away to each other and to the aides, who responded with good humor but scant attention.

A woman and her little girl walked toward us. The child, about six, stared. She seemed curious rather than disturbed or repelled. I was getting ready to say hello to her as we passed but her mother grabbed her arm and crossed the street, looking back at us with plain dislike. The old pain and anger rose in me. Bill and the others waved and smiled at the little girl, now across the road. She waved back.

The aides led us down the hill, stopping the traffic as our line of cripples filed over the zebra crossing. It was a Saturday afternoon and the playground was full of shrieking children. We parked ourselves in front of a couple of benches and watched the kids laughing, jumping, climbing the fanciful wooden structures. You can enjoy that sight a lot, even if you can't jump and play yourself. Your body feels itself stretching and lifting, it feels the thrill of being up high or swinging in an arc, back and forth, back and forth. The children's cheeks were red. Some of them had pulled off their puffy jackets and thrown them on the ground.

Three children, two boys and a girl about nine, were throwing a ball in the cricket pitch. It came sailing towards us and one of the other men caught it with a yell. He threw it back to them. The girl threw it to him again.

"What's your name?" she shouted as the ball flew between them.

"Freddie! What's yours?"

"Excuse me." Two young women were speaking to the aides. They had pushchairs with bundled-up babies in them. "We need to use these benches. Could you take them somewhere else, please?"

"That's all right!" called Bill. "We don't mind. Sorry!"

The women glanced at him and quickly away back to the aides, who shrugged.

"Come on!" said Bill to the rest of us. "They need the benches for the babies!" He paused to smile and coo down at one of them, who looked back with an unblinking stare then burst into a grin.

"I mean, sorry, we don't want to make you leave but…" said the baby's mother.

"Lovely baby," said Bill. He wheeled himself away. The others followed.

Wendy rolled up beside me so that I could see what she'd typed on her board. "What would Virginia Woolf say?"

I didn't know what she was talking about. Back in her room at Three Wells she tapped at her computer until she found what she wanted. It was a page from her thesis about attitudes to disability in literature.

Her finger pointed shakily to a quote from Virginia Woolf's diary.

"'On the towpath we met & had to pass a long line of imbeciles,'" I read aloud. I frowned at Wendy and went on. "'...& then one realised that every one in that long line was a miserable ineffective shuffling idiotic creature with no forehead, or no chin, & an imbecile grin, or a wild suspicious stare. It was perfectly horrible. They should certainly be killed.'"

Virginia Woolf, spokeswoman for women's rights, wanted people like us to be eliminated. She wouldn't have known or cared who we were as human beings. Our wheelchairs and our deformed bodies and our defective speech would have told her enough.

Fifty years was not so long ago. Did people still think like that? The women with their babies, the mother of the six-year old?

I wished I was like Bill and the others, who'd figured out what to do in the face of prejudice.

I thought about it a lot in the next few days—why disabled bodies are so repulsive and frightening for ordinary people. "What if it's some kind of evolutionary instinct?" I wrote to Wendy the next day. "We threaten the survival of the group. We can't get up and run away from danger. And we might have dodgy genes. Best to avoid us or destroy us."

And then I started thinking about the opposite—how ordinary people respond to physical perfection. Did human beauty promise the flourishing of the species? Is that why people adored movie stars and beauty queens? I thought of

Diana, of course. She'd been on the news the night before, doing a walkabout somewhere in the north. The camera went back and forth from her to the people she was greeting on the street. They were not ill or disabled. But nor were they tall and beautiful, straight-backed and perfectly groomed like her. They were shorter, older, fatter, with poorly kept hair, false teeth, dowdy clothes, the hard, wrinkled mouths of smokers. I saw their faces lit with Diana's loveliness. It was as though she showed them a sort of idealized mirror of themselves. She was generous with her beauty, she let other people take it on as their own. She did not keep it for herself alone, the way other beautiful people did.

The same thing happened with the landmine victims, the AIDS patients, the people with leprosy. Ill, injured, or damaged, they felt redeemed by her health and beauty. As I had. For the few minutes of our dance, I, crippled Alex, was mobile and graceful. Even now, once in a great while, I could summon the sense of that grace and movement in my body.

CHAPTER FOURTEEN

August 30, 1997, evening

She wakes up, chilled, and switches on the light. Almost nine o'clock. She remembers the nightclub and groans, wishing again that she could just sleep until it was time to go home. But her lover is refreshed after his nap. "No, no, no," he cries gaily, leaping up and running around the bed. He pulls her playfully to her feet. "The night is just beginning! We'll have fun, darling. And we need dinner. Put that sexy black dress on again."

But the moment for the sexy dress is past. She chooses instead a black linen jacket and slim white trousers. He is disappointed and she is not sorry.

It doesn't matter what she wears. She is aware that she looks perfect in anything. It is not a cause for vanity, but a kind of comfort. In Angola a few months ago, she let them—willingly—film her in plain khakis and a sleeveless shirt, driving in a dusty jeep, striding along sandy roads, carrying nothing, accompanied by men who were not lovers or equerries, who welcomed and respected her because of the support she could offer to their cause. She'd been briefed before going but was devastated by the reality—thousands of people, many of them women and children, arms and legs torn off by treacherous mines buried in the fields where they grew food and played. She'd never seen or imagined so many people on crutches. The luckier few had prosthetic limbs, for which they had had to wait years.

The wounds she saw in the hospitals were appalling. She made herself look, so that the cameras would go where her eyes went and then others, far away, would see too. They brought her to a seven-year-old girl whose intestines had been blasted out of her body. The child lay passively in the crowded clinic, her threadbare dress raised to display the enormous wound, her small private parts exposed as well. She held the little girl's unresisting hand as the medical people explained in quiet voices. As soon as she could she took the sheet and covered the child's lower body, then caressed the small braided head lightly.

"How does one survive an injury like that?" she said to her host later, touching her own side. He looked at her and said nothing, and she understood that the little girl would not live, that she was in fact dying.

She loved that child, whom she'd only just met and would never see again. She loved the one-legged boy in the next bed, and the woman who sat motionless on the doorstep, both arms ending in rag-wrapped stumps. She couldn't heal them but she loved them. She knew they felt it.

This is my work, she thinks now, sitting up straighter as the car speeds towards the nightclub. I have to do more. It's exactly the right moment, with Labour and their charismatic leader now in power, promising bold new changes. Back in January, while she was in Angola, someone in Parliament had referred to her as a loose cannon. But the Labour MPs had applauded her. When they won the election she'd thought: Yes! Now! Hugh, operating in the deep waters of the civil service, had encouraged her and promised to help. "It's perfect for you, duckie," he said. "You can do it. Not a doubt in my mind."

She believes both that she can do it and that she cannot.

The loose cannon remark stings her still. I am not a loose cannon, she thinks. I've done some truly idiotic things in my life. That I have. But I'm not a fool. She is deathly tired of being dismissed as beautiful but stupid, or, worse, out of her mind.

She is suddenly nauseated with herself, riding in leather-seated luxury to a Paris nightclub with a wealthy boyfriend caressing her leg. She doesn't belong here. She belongs with people who are suffering. She belongs with her own children. She adores being with her children. She doesn't care that her ex-husband's family thinks she is too involved as a parent, too indulgent. Their idea of a mother is a woman who could leave her small child for four months and then greet him with a solemn handshake, in front of hundreds of onlookers. No hugs, no kisses for the little chap, who was himself now the loudest voice of criticism.

When she was a bride she had briefly tried to squeeze a little motherliness out of her mother-in-law—surely that soft skin, that ample chest hid a mother's heart, however buried. She yearned for it and felt she could unlock it with her youthful sincerity. Now that was truly idiotic, she concedes to herself, looking back.

She feels a spike of childish longing for her own mother, who is on the other side of the world in her new life, barely in touch.

The car swerves and she is thrown against the door. She is not wearing a seatbelt. "Sorry, your Highness," says the driver.

The photographers on their motorbikes have surrounded the car. She is suddenly distraught.

"Let's not go to the club!" she cries to her lover. "They'll follow us inside—they'll ruin it."

He is imperturbable. "Where do you want to go, darling?"

But she has no answer. Her elation of a few minutes ago is gone and she is fighting tears again. He tells the driver to turn around, take them back to the hotel. "We'll have some dinner, sweetheart. Nice quiet dinner and some more champagne."

She has no appetite at all but it is better to be safe inside the restaurant than out here on the street, exposed to hundreds of greedy eyes and the assault of flashing cameras.

Why must I be all these different people, she thinks in despair. Why can't I be just one person, like other people, like Abdel the driver with his broad shoulders and steady hands. He probably has a home, a wife and children. He doesn't have a wardrobe of selves that he must shuffle and choose from constantly. He is just Abdel.

I want to be just my real self, she thinks. If only I can work out who that is.

CHAPTER FIFTEEN

Alex

I was very worried about Diana. By now she and Charles were legally separated. I'd finally had to concede that the fairytale was a pretense and always had been. Or rather, if it was a fairytale, it was the dark and frightening kind, not the happy-ever-after kind.

When a new biography was touted as a clandestine collaboration between Diana and the author I did not believe it. She would never expose her troubles in this way. The author had made up the sordid, depressing details with the help of self-serving rumormongers and gossips. I maintained a personal boycott of the book, which was on view everywhere, displayed in shop windows and the library, pictured in newspaper and magazine ads week after week, with Diana looking very glamorous and princess-y on the cover.

My father brought up the subject when I went to visit him and Jess in Exeter.

"I had a look at your heartthrob's book," said my father. He still had fun teasing me about Diana, though he didn't know the real reason for my interest in her. We were sitting at an outdoor café across the green from the cathedral. A guide and her cluster of tourists gazed up at the hideous gargoyles under the roof. "What a display, eh?"

"It's not Diana's book. She didn't write it," I said. "And she's not my heartthrob. Anyway I haven't read it."

"Well, don't, if you want to hold onto your fantasy," said my father. He took a handful of peanuts and tossed them into his mouth like an elephant. "Because she comes off as a dimwitted, narcissistic little fruitcake. And her over-privileged pals—Jesus, what a crowd. Too much money for their own good, nothing on their minds except the next party and who's bedding who."

"I skimmed it," said Jess. "My sister's reading it. Honestly, Alex, I don't think she's someone you'd get along with if you actually knew her."

From what I'd heard, the book seemed to be about someone altogether different from the woman in my private dreams. I picked up my drink carefully and had a sip. Not a good moment to spill Guinness down my shirt. "Maybe. But it can't be the whole story, can it? If she was that vapid, why would millions and millions of people love her? They're not all stupid. I'm not stupid. As you know."

It took a while to get this little speech out. I drank some more beer.

"Well. Anyway," said Jess. "Have a peanut. Shall we go and have a look at the cathedral?"

I wished I could talk to them about the worst fear that the book aroused in me. Apparently the writer described not only Diana's husband's infidelities but her own. If any of it was true, it wasn't her fault. She'd been manipulated into an impossible situation, then exploited and betrayed. No wonder she turned her despair onto herself, and then reached out rashly to others in hopes that they could make her feel better.

The trouble for me was that she seemed to like handsome men in uniform. I was still tortured by the memory of her hand on Adam Widmer's arm years ago, her face smiling up into his. I could not bear the idea of a romantic connection between Diana and this man whom I considered an unpunished murderer. As far as I knew the book didn't name her lovers. I had to try and convince myself that although she might have fallen in love with men like Adam, she did not fall in love with him.

I watched Diana's BBC interview a couple of years later from a hospital bed after a particularly bad seizure. Dr. Barrow's successor—he was long retired—kept trying new medications but none of them worked for long. I was drained like a butchered lamb afterwards, a feeble thread of a person, barely enough strength to open my eyes. When I did, Gillian was there. My mother had told her that I was ill and she'd insisted on coming immediately, all the way from London and her busy job.

"Gillian," I said. I wasn't up to saying much. She smiled and some of the shadow left her face. She reached out and took my hand. The room was quiet except for beeping machines. The other bed was empty. "You look horrible," she said. She, on the other hand, looked terrific. She was wearing a smoky-blue cardigan that matched her eyes. Her earrings were the same color. I felt again the old pride and wanted to announce, look, this is my sister, I have a sister who is beautiful and perfect.

After a while they brought dinner. Everything was white—mashed potatoes, white fish, white bread, an indefinable white pudding. I took a few mouthfuls and stopped. Gillian didn't press me to eat more.

"Tell me how you are," I said. I didn't feel like talking but I wanted to listen.

She understood. I closed my eyes, feeling her hand in mine. It was like having a bedtime story. She talked about her job, helping to administer projects dealing with child poverty and disease. She described her new flat, which she shared with someone called Kamala from India, her co-worker at the children's organization. "You'll meet her sometime," she said. "Kamala's fabulous."

Then she said: "Alex—I don't know if you're up to it, but we could turn on the tv. Do you know about Diana's interview?"

I did know about it but I'd forgotten. An electrical storm in your brain will knock things out of your mind, no matter how important they are. Now I remembered. Apparently Diana had recorded a long, revealing interview which Buckingham Palace had not seen or approved and was not going to like at all. No one in the royal family had ever released an interview unvetted by the palace. But Diana was barely part of that family any more.

"It's on tonight?" I said.

Gillian nodded. She looked at her watch. "Couple of minutes."

I pushed at the tray. "Get rid…"

Gillian wheeled it aside and switched on the television. They began with shots of Diana at her most gorgeous and triumphant, in one spectacular dress after another. Then they switched to a sitting room in Kensington Palace where she sat unsmiling in a somber outfit, looking tense but composed. She tipped her head down and looked up at the interviewer from the corners of her huge dark-smudged eyes as if begging his forbearance. Her words came readily but after every response she held her breath—"Did I really just say that? Was that OK?"

I hated to see her like this. To hear her litany of disappointments, wounds, humiliations, misjudgments, losses. I ached for all that she'd endured, and for the indignity of this moment, ripping herself open for all to see. She spoke about realizing that her husband loved someone else and probably always had. She talked without embarrassment about her own romances. "Yes, I adored him," she said, speaking of someone who could have been, but was not, thank god, Adam.

I wanted to protest: this is not who she really is! No! Not who she was meant to be! The real Diana was the girl I'd met at fifteen, who danced with a disabled boy and gave him joy, and grew up to give joy to thousands of others. That was my Diana. Not this pitiable figure with her proud words and her pleading eyes. "I'd like to be a queen of people's hearts," she was saying wistfully. "Well, you are! You are!" I wanted to shout at her.

Gillian glanced at me and handed me a tissue from the night table. She helped herself to a tissue as well.

When it was over she switched off the set. Neither of us had any stomach for the chorus of reactions and instant analysis. I felt exhausted and sad. "I'll be back tomorrow," Gillian said. She kissed my cheek and left.

I feared for Diana after that. I thought maybe she was done for, too damaged to recover. But she did recover. As did I. My strength returned quickly, surprising the doctors and my family.

Diana seemed to grow steadily more robust over the next year. She looked healthier, more relaxed, more athletic. The gossip about romantic foolishness continued but there were also more and more stories about traveling to obscure places where people were suffering, using that mysterious ability she had to make an instant, heartfelt link with a stranger. I was proud of her, and relieved.

She flew to New York to receive a humanitarian award from a big cerebral palsy organization. I watched a few minutes of her speech on the news, waiting for her to say: "Years ago, when I was a schoolgirl myself, I visited a school for boys with cerebral palsy. I danced with a boy in a wheelchair. I've never forgotten it. And I've often wondered about that boy's life." She said nothing of the kind, of course.

A year and a half after that awful interview the BBC showed something entirely different, a documentary about Diana in Angola with victims of landmines. She narrated it herself. She seemed so direct and so strong, striding along in her khakis, sitting with dreadfully wounded children and adults, posing with her arms around kids on crutches. It was brilliant, using the media's obsession with her to make the world pay attention to the atrocity of landmines. No one watching could ever forget.

To me it looked like Diana's future, this trip and the film about it. She seemed so at home, visiting the crowded clinics, talking with people and comforting them, and then reporting on it to make everyone else understand. It seemed clear where she would go from there. Clear to me, anyway.

CHAPTER SIXTEEN

August 30, 1997, evening

The Mercedes sits in traffic two blocks from the hotel. She thinks again about those visits to her mother when she was six years old, when her mother lived in a flat instead of their big house, with only a few rooms all on the same floor. She would go there with her brother or her older sisters. The flat was too small for them all to visit together. There was a back garden that all the flats shared, but it wasn't very big and most of the time it wasn't sunny. It had a swing with a crooked seat that left a patch of damp on the back of her dress when she sat on it.

She loved and hated the visits. She loved seeing her mother, running into her arms, feeling her, smelling her again, nestling beside her to read stories, playing Snakes and Ladders on the tapestry-covered footstool in front of the couch. But it made her sad to see her mother in this strange place, which was not their home. Her mother didn't belong there. Her mother was too pretty to live in a poky flat. Sometimes her mother's friend was there too, a kind man, but usually her mother was alone. She understood that Daddy was angry at Mummy, and that made her sad too. Everyone was angry with her mother, even her grandmothers, both of them. When they spoke of her they frowned as though her mother had done something very naughty indeed and must be punished. "Poor Mummy," she said to her sisters. "It's not fair." She felt sorry for her. But her sisters said it was Mummy's fault that everything was so different.

Her brother was too little to think about whose fault it was, so she liked going to visit with him better than with her sisters. Until that moment when they had to put on their coats and their gloves and get ready to say goodbye to their mother. "But we want to stay with you, Mummy!" she begged. Her little brother wailed along with her. "No, darlings," her mother said, unhooking their arms from around her, pretending that everything was all right. "No, darlings, you must go home to Daddy."

"But why? Don't you want us?"

At that her mother's face crumpled and she held both of them so tightly in her arms that they could hardly breathe. "You must go home to Daddy." At the railway station her mother didn't look at them any more and was mean to the nanny who came to take them back.

One night in the flat she lay scrunched in bed in her new nightdress with the rosebuds on it, trying to go to sleep, dreading the next day when they would have to leave. Her little brother was sound asleep in the next bed. She didn't want to wake him. The pillow was getting wet with her tears but her crying was almost silent. Her throat ached. It wasn't fair. Why couldn't her mother and father love each other, the way they used to? Why did she and her brother and sisters always have to say goodbye and leave? She wanted to howl loudly but knew she mustn't. And then she realized that she was hearing someone else's soft crying. She looked over at her brother. He hadn't moved. She crept out of bed and tiptoed along the hall to her mother's room. The light beside the bed was on. Her mother lay curled on top of her bed in her clothes. Her shoes lay tumbled across each other on the floor and her stockinged feet looked cold. Her mother's face was pressed into the pillow. Her body shook and heaved.

"Mummy!" she whispered. She wasn't sure if her mother heard her. She reached out and patted her arm. Her mother didn't seem to notice. So she climbed up onto the bed and cradled her mother's head in her arms, stroking her hair back from her forehead, dropping little kisses onto her cheeks. "There, there," she crooned. "There, there, dear. Don't cry." Her mother stiffened for a moment, then nestled into her. After a while her sobs subsided into long shuddering sighs.

She bent over her mother, holding and soothing her. A sweet peacefulness suffused her and she felt comforted herself.

The Mercedes jolts and moves ahead slowly. She wonders if her mother remembers that moment. It seems unlikely. It has been so long, she thinks, since we held each other like that. They won, all those people who wanted to get her out of our lives.

CHAPTER SEVENTEEN

Alex

In October I got an invitation that I had wanted and dreaded since I began visiting schools. Westerford Comprehensive asked me to come and speak. I said yes, I'd be happy to come, ignoring the immediate churning in my entrails.

"We understand that you attended our school, Mr. Carr," said the headmistress on the phone. "And that you were a pupil here at the time of a tragedy that may possibly have been related to bullying."

May have been related! Well, they'd find out just how related it was.

I wanted Jane to come with me. She was pleased that I was going but she wasn't sure that she could face it herself. "I've grown a lot of scar tissue," she said when we met to talk about it. "Probably not a good idea to tear it off."

I wasn't exactly sure why I wanted her to come, but I did. Michele's mother and Michele's friend, telling her story, finally, if not to the perpetrators and passive witnesses, then to their successors. Not just for Michele's sake, or for ours, but for the disabled kids who were at the school now and probably suffered more than the adults knew, even though, according to the headmistress, things were much better than in our day. I knew from all my school visits that school bullying was alive and well. Handicapped kids were still easy targets.

It was this thought that persuaded Jane—that our visit might help those young people.

My mother wanted to come too. I objected at first, but she wasn't coming to protect me. She wanted to witness this moment of redress. As we hoped it would be.

I'd passed by the school gates many times with no desire to enter. As we drove up the hill I wanted to tell my mother to keep going. But she turned in and parked in a space marked "Visitor." I am a visitor, I told myself. I'll leave again in an hour or so and never come back unless I want to. There was now a ramp up to the main door, I was pleased to see. My bones and muscles remembered the slow climb with my crutches, levering my weight upwards, trying to ignore the other kids bounding up two steps at a time, praying that they wouldn't pause to taunt me.

At the top of the ramp the headmistress was waiting with a smile of welcome. I introduced her to Jane and my mother, pretending that it felt perfectly normal to be here as a respected guest. She held the front door open for us. The echo of shoes on the tiled floor, the paneled walls, the photos of old sports teams and portraits of earlier headmasters, the intimidating aura of authority—it was all profoundly familiar. But I was different. I was no longer the small, barely-pubescent teenager slinking around the periphery, hoping not to be noticed. I was an adult. I was here because I chose to be. I could leave whenever I wanted. No one was going to hurt me.

Jane and my mother stayed close by. I was grateful.

The headmistress escorted us toward the hall. She pointed out the classroom doors, now wide enough for wheelchairs. "We have four pupils currently who are wheelchair-bound," she said over her shoulder. It seemed to be a source of pride.

My thirteen-year-old self swung along on his sticks as close to the wall as he could, a girl in callipers beside him carrying his books, the two of them talking nonstop as though they did not notice the sneering looks and comments. Their vulnerability pierced me, and their defiance, their separateness and solidarity.

Michele had been destroyed. But I'd escaped. I'd survived. I'd made a life for myself, a reasonably good life, of which our former schoolmates knew nothing. I wished passionately that I could walk beside those two brave children, shielding them, telling them that school would not last forever.

The headmistress led us onto the stage of the big hall. The teachers were already seated along the back. I nodded to them. One, a man about my age, smiled as though he knew me. I looked out at the rows of young people in their school uniforms, chattering and fidgeting. I had a moment of abject terror, as though it was twenty years ago and I'd suddenly found myself on the stage by mistake. Adam and his henchmen were out there. Any second the jeering would begin. "Spit-and-dribble!" I would hear. "Cripple! Whatcha doing here, anyway? Give us a song and dance!" I yanked myself back to the present. In the front row were the disabled children. One boy caught my eye and we exchanged a split-second smile of complicity. The room quietened. Jane and I sat while the headmistress introduced us both. My mother stood in the back of the hall.

I wheeled forward to the microphone. Fear shook me once more. I wanted very badly to disappear before they made me regret my audacity. But I had waited so long to tell the truth in the place where it mattered the most.

My nerve came back.

"Good morning, everyone. My name is Alex Carr." They had just heard my name from the headmistress but I wanted them to adjust to my slow speech. "I talk like this because I have cerebral palsy. My legs don't work very well, also because of cerebral palsy, so I have to use a wheelchair." I looked at them. They seemed to be listening. "Can you understand me all right?"

"Yes!" a few voices called out.

I didn't have notes. I knew what I wanted to say.

"I went to this school many years ago. There was a lot of bullying at that time. Anyone who was different in any way was likely to get bullied. If you were poor, or fat. If they thought you were a sissy. Being disabled made you a target." I took a deep breath. "I left when I was fourteen because my friend Michele was bullied to death."

There was an audible gasp. Out of the corner of my eye I saw the headmistress make a move toward me, then stop. Too bad, I thought, I've got the microphone. I'd never talked to kids in this way before, deliberately shocking them at the outset. But this was different. This was the scene of the crime. I wanted every boy and every girl in that room to remember what I was going to say. Every adult as well.

"Michele wasn't as disabled as me. She also had cerebral palsy but she could walk OK with callipers. She talked normally. She was funny and bright and pretty, and she was very good at art." I could see her right there, sitting in the front row, looking mightily embarrassed, wondering what I was going to say next.

"How many of you went to Eastcott?" A number of hands went up. "That's where we met each other, Michele and I. We were the first disabled children who went there, the two of us and a couple of others. The other pupils weren't used to seeing handicapped children. There were some boys, one in particular, who didn't like us. I don't know why they hated us so much."

I looked around at the boys and girls, seeing them properly as themselves, not as my schoolmates from long ago. Some looked like children. Others were young adults already, boys with broad shoulders, girls with fashionable hairdos. I had no idea who they were, what their lives were like. Who was mean, who was vulnerable.

"This one particular boy and his friends tormented us for years, at Eastcott and then here at Westerford Comprehensive. Every day they made us feel frightened and ashamed. Sometimes they kicked or hit us. Nobody stopped them, neither the teachers nor the headmaster nor the other kids."

I had their attention. They were waiting to find out how Michele was bullied to death.

So I told them. I didn't use Adam's name, but I said what he was like, athletic and good-looking and popular. And brutal. I told them what he did to Michele, how he made her feel so dreadfully exposed and ashamed, and how it crushed her. My words were slow as always but not hesitant. I felt unstoppable, like the river when the tide flows in. I made them see what I saw. It was all so vivid in my mind, being back here in the school, as if it had been only weeks instead of more than twenty years.

"The headmaster at that time said he was sorry but he couldn't do anything about it. He didn't want to confront the boy or talk to his parents. So the boy got away with it scot free. He killed my friend, he killed Jane's daughter—" I looked at her— "and he never got caught or punished.

"So I left. I didn't want to be here any more. I went to boarding school. This is the first time I've been back. Thank you for inviting me."

The young people sat still for a moment and then broke into subdued applause. I glanced back at Jane. She looked pale but she nodded. I beckoned her forward. She stood beside me. I reached up and grasped her hand. At this point I didn't care what anyone thought. My job was almost done. I breathed out. I asked if anyone had a question, for either of us.

A boy who looked about fifteen raised his hand and stood up when I nodded to him.

"This isn't a question," he said. "I just want to say that I'm really sorry about Michele." He paused. "That's all." He sat down amid a murmur of agreement.

Hands started waving urgently. Questions for Jane— "Did your daughter tell you what was going on?" "Did you go to the police?"—and questions for me, or both of us.

We had about ten minutes left. One more thing I had to do.

"My turn to ask a question," I said. "Do you think something like that could happen here now?"

None of the disabled girls and boys had so far spoken up. I saw them react to my question, but they stayed quiet.

The able-bodied kids were eager to answer. No, they said, no, it couldn't possibly happen now. No one would be so cruel, and if they were, the teachers would make them stop. The young people were indignant at the idea. They wanted to distance themselves from the perpetrators in my story. No! We would never be like that!

I looked again at the boys and girls in wheelchairs in the front row and the other disabled kids beside them, more mobile but marked by differences—a strange posture, a clunky hearing aid. Sitting together, no doubt, because they were grouped together in a special room. "What do you think?" I asked them directly. "Could someone get bullied here because they're handicapped?"

They glanced at each other, self-conscious. A girl in a wheelchair with bright eyes and short blond hair looked straight at me. The kids on either side of her poked her. She raised her hand.

"Yes," she said. "It happens every day. Not as bad as for you, though."

I heard a little sound of dismay from the headmistress behind us.

"What's your name?" I asked the girl.

"Bronwen Farrelly."

I invited her to come onto the stage and say more. She hesitated, then wheeled herself to the ramp on the side. Another girl jumped up to help push her. Bronwen flashed her a smile.

It was probably the first time in the school's history that there were two wheelchairs on the stage of the big hall. I was going to wring every drop I could out of this moment. Michele, I thought, are you watching?

Jane gave Bronwen the other microphone.

"Say anything you want," I said. I realized my own heart was thumping, as though I was a teenager again and had been given a chance to speak, with everyone listening. I willed her to have courage.

"Well. OK," Bronwen said. "This happened yesterday." She waited. Tell them, tell them, Bronwen, I begged silently, knowing how extremely hard it was for her to keep going. She took a breath and went on. "A person bumped into my friend in the corridor, on purpose. She almost fell. She dropped her books on the floor and he laughed at her. He said she couldn't read them anyway because she was a moron. It's hard for her to bend down and I couldn't help because of my wheelchair. He—he stared at her bending over…" Bronwen stopped. She wasn't going to say any more.

There was complete silence.

A girl sitting near the back put up her hand. "It's true. I saw it happen. He always does it."

I turned to glance at the headmistress. She shook her head, looking stern. I will deal with this, she meant. Or that's what I hoped she meant.

My energy was draining rapidly. I wanted the other kids to hear Bronwen say one more thing. "Bronwen." I gestured toward the girl who'd spoken up. "What could she have done to help? Or anyone else who witnessed something like this?"

Bronwen didn't hesitate. "Just tell that boy to stop. And if he doesn't, get a teacher." She looked at the audience. "And make friends with us, we're not weirdos."

Someone started clapping and others joined in. There were cheers. Bronwen looked astonished. What a great kid, I was thinking. Who wouldn't want to be friends with her?

"OK," I said. My amplified voice cut through the cheering. Brilliant, the power you have with a microphone. "Everyone. If you think you could do what Bronwen said next time you see someone getting bullied—please stand up!"

The headmistress was probably afraid I was starting a riot

but I didn't care. One boy stood up, then another, then a couple of girls, and then a tumble of others until three quarters of the kids were on their feet, clapping and whistling. Hundreds of them. Smiling, Bronwen raised her fist like a Black Panther.

My heart was flying around the arched ceiling. Michele, Michele. Look at them. They would have stood up for us too.

I wasn't fooling myself that this roomful of ordinary kids had suddenly become heroes. But in that moment they meant it. Something had shifted for them.

The bell rang and the pupils poured out of the hall. The headmistress thanked me and Jane, polite but reserved. I wasn't sure how pleased she was. I hoped she'd at least look into what Bronwen had said.

I was shaken by all of it. Literally trembling. Most of the teachers rushed off to their classes but a few paused to speak to us. "Thank you, Mr. Carr—may I call you Alex?" "So badly needed." "We would love you to make a yearly visit, if you were willing." I nodded and smiled and shook hands but I needed urgently to get out. Jane and my mother were edging me toward the front door as fast as they could. Another teacher hurried up to us. It was the man who'd smiled at me when we arrived on the stage.

"Alex," he said, shaking my hand. "Jeff Hazelwood. I don't think you remember me. We were at school here together." I had a vague memory of a boy in my science class. Not one of the bullies, I was certain. "Anyway," he said. "Thank you for coming here. I'm sorry about what you went through." He paused and lowered his voice. "The person you were referring to? I didn't know about all of that, what he was doing to you and Michele. But he wasn't as popular as you might have thought. Something about him. I kept a distance, and so did my friends." He shook his head. "I promise you I'll do all I can, personally, to make sure nothing like that ever happens again. We all will, I hope."

I hoped so too.

When we got to the car I ejected myself from my wheelchair and flopped into the back seat. I was spent. My mother folded up the chair and packed it in the boot.

"Lordy," she said as we drove out of the gates. "That was absolutely terrific, Alex. You too, Jane. My god. I wish..." She didn't finish. I knew what she was thinking.

"But we might have saved someone else's life today," Jane said slowly. "There's no way of knowing. If only we could tell Michele."

All these years I'd wanted justice for Michele. I'd thought that meant Adam finally getting the exposure and punishment he deserved. In the weeks after visiting the school, that impotent, enraged yearning slowly ebbed away. I had told Michele's story in the place where it happened. Bronwen's voice had been heard. We had enlisted hundreds of girls and boys and their teachers to stand up against another Adam. He himself might be oblivious, but the field had shifted. It changed the past as well as the present.

CHAPTER EIGHTEEN

August 30, 1997, evening

Her lover's mobile phone rings. He reaches into his soft black leather purse, glancing apologetically at her. It is his father. He speaks in Arabic for a few minutes and hangs up.

"Sorry, sweetheart. He just wanted to know if we're all right. He said to give you his love."

"What did you tell him?"

"I said we're fine, we're having fun! He asked if they'd put the champagne in our room."

His father is worried, she thinks. He's noticed, even if his son has not, that she's pulling away from them. She's not the grateful, amenable person she was at the beginning of their jaunt around the Mediterranean. He'd lock us in that hotel suite if he could, she thinks, he'd force his son to propose and me to accept. Like one of those kings in a fairytale who kidnaps potential brides for his son, and kills the ones who don't cooperate. The press used to call her life a fairytale. Yes, it was, perhaps, but not in the Disney way they meant. Fairytales are full of revenge and violence and gruesome punishments. She thinks of the ugly sisters doomed to dance forever in red-hot iron shoes. The bad fairy who condemned a whole country to a hundred-year coma because she was not invited to the royal christening.

The bad fairy in her own story was not excluded from the festivities although she, the bride, would have preferred her to be. She squatted like a toad in her pew, biding her time. She did not have to wait long.

In the car she is seized with homesickness and takes out her own phone. It's far too late at night to call but she tries anyway. She hears the phone ringing and imagines it echoing in the stone hallways of a Highland castle. No one answers. Her ex-husband's family would not, of course, use something as banal as an answer machine. She lets it ring many times, then hangs up. Her boys are no doubt sound asleep, happily tired after another day of chasing deer and trout. They enjoy it, she knows, impenetrable as those pastimes are to her. Once, long ago, she'd been happy in that Highlands retreat too, in the fleeting time of grace when her new husband had seemed enchanted with her. She'd actually tried wielding a fishing rod, his arms around her to guide her, his laughter at her lack of skill affectionate, not mocking. Her sons were good at fishing, at riding and hunting. They were his sons too. Of course. But hers most of all.

Her lover pats her hand, sympathetic. "You'll see them soon. They'll be so happy to be with mama again."

She tries not to sink into the hollowness inside her. She'll see her boys, and it will be lovely, but then they'll go off to school again, and what else does she have to look forward to? She's growing pessimistic now about the bold plan that she plotted with Hugh. She had persuaded herself, and him, that it could work. Another delusion, she fears.

There's a trip to Thailand coming up, with an AIDS organization, or is it landmines again, she's not certain. Her calendar is full of appearances in England as well, her usual charities. I want something bigger, she thinks. I'm ready to do more. Let me take my proper place!

She's been dreaming about making more films like the one about Angola. If her lover was a different kind of person she might even invite him to get involved, with his connections in the film world. But making documentaries to relieve suffering does not interest him at all.

They'd argued about her trip to Bosnia, just a couple of weeks ago. Sunning on the deck after a swim she had reminded him that she was to go the following week.

He put down his vodka and tonic. "You didn't tell me!" he cried.

"I did," she said. "It's been on my calendar for ages. I'll be with the landmine people. I'm going to meet some of the victims and families." The thought stirred her. She was eager to be there. "It's just for three days." She caressed the inside of his arm to console him.

"But I've invited Randy and Alicia! They're longing to see you again. I promised them!" He was dreadfully disappointed, like a child. Randy and Alicia, Hollywood's current darlings, were pictured on glossy magazine covers almost as often as herself. She found she couldn't muster much interest.

"I'm sorry. I have to go." How could she explain to him that she must go? The more she sank into this cushioned life the more she felt an urgency to be in that other world where survival itself mattered. Where her other self lived.

"But why do you want to be with people you don't even know instead of my friends?"

She saw that he was truly hurt and upset. “I’m sorry, darling.” She leaned over to him and kissed his thick eyebrows, one and then the other. “I’ll come back very soon.”

Arriving in Sarajevo was like awakening abruptly from a drugged sleep. They drove her to the countryside in a battered van with windows that did not roll up all the way. Her hair blew in all directions. She laughed, trying to hold it down with her hands. The green hills and fields looked peaceful, the limb-shattering bombs out of sight under shallow earth. A few cameras—invited reporters, not paparazzi—followed her to the front doors of village houses where inside she had long conversations alone with the family and a translator.

She was not famous here. They knew only that she was interested in their plight and she could make others interested too. She felt at ease with families where one or more members were missing limbs, like in Angola. Putting her arm around a shoulder, joking and cuddling with a child, even watching the strange fierceness of a ballgame played by men without legs, and sitting with them afterwards on the stained floor of the gym to hear their stories—it all felt natural to her. This is what I do.

And then the graveyard on a hill with far too many fresh graves, where she met the woman who had lost her son. They held each other and wept for all the lost sons.

Tears prick her eyes again as she remembers, tears for the grieving woman or for herself, or both.

The car waits at an intersection. Pedestrians hurry across the road, people on their way home, or seeking Saturday night amusement. A tall black man and a short white woman walk entwined, not minding the rain. She feels strained, her nerves stretched to breaking. The day is interminable.

CHAPTER NINETEEN

Alex

Gillian kept urging me to come and see her in London. "Do come, Alex. We'd love to have you. We'll take you anywhere. Do you want to visit Kensington Palace?"

"We" meant the girl she shared her flat with, Kamala. I was curious to meet her. My mother, finally, seemed to accept that I could handle a trip without her. The journey was awkward but manageable. I ignored the occasional unsympathetic look and found a couple of kind people who didn't mind helping me when I had to change trains.

Gillian met me at Paddington, conspicuous in a colorful shawl. With her travels she'd acquired a collection of exotic garments and jewelry that she combined with her more sober gear to great effect. She waved and jumped up and down like a kid, running to hug me and help me down to the platform. "This is my brother Alex!" she said. Another young woman waited nearby, similar to Gillian in her neat small shape and her vivid smile. She looked Indian. She shook my hand warmly.

"Alex, this is Kamala," said Gillian. "I told you about her."

"So happy to meet you at last, Alex." She seemed friendly but formal.

They swept me away to their flat on the ground floor of a small building in south London. My chair fit through the front door with a centimeter to spare. With some maneuvering they got me into the living room. Art gallery posters decorated pale green walls. There was a folded mattress on the floor— "A futon," Gillian said. "We'll open it up for you to sleep on." Books were everywhere, on shelves, on the coffee table, stacked on the floor. Coppery flowers in a glass vase. In the corner there was a basket with balls of wool and someone's knitting rolled up on thick needles. So this was my little sister's home. It seemed cozy and busy, a place where girls lived, not boys.

Kamala came back into the living room with a tray of tea things and put it on the table. They stood there smiling at me, arms linked.

"Come on, we'll show you around," said Gillian. The flat was tiny. "This is our room." I looked into a small room with Indian silk fabrics draped on the walls. One large bed. Gillian turned and put her arm around Kamala, who was standing right behind us in the narrow hallway. "Kamala's my sweetheart. We're together."

It took me a moment to comprehend. I knew some gay people in the disability crowd and in my mother's circle of friends. It just hadn't occurred to me that Gillian would fall for a girl rather than a boy. But I liked the idea that she loved someone. Kamala seemed quite lovable, as was Gillian herself, of course.

After dinner we talked about it. Kamala had gone out to a meeting. "Are Mum and Dad going to freak out when I tell them?" Gillian asked.

I thought they'd be surprised, as I was, and then they'd be fine. "Dad might have some complaints but Jess'll sort him out."

"She will," said Gillian. "I'm dying to bring Kamala down to Devon."

I was in London for four days, the first two by myself until Gillian and Kamala came home from work. I loved it. I figured out how to eject myself onto the street, locking the heavy door behind me as though I'd lived in a Wandsworth flat all my life. I wheeled around the noisy streets amongst more people than I'd ever seen in my life. People of all ages and colors, some in the clothes of Africa or Asia or the Middle East. I felt like a twig tossed into a swirling torrent of humanity. No one paid attention to me. Occasionally I saw someone else in a wheelchair or riding a little electric scooter and we'd acknowledge each other with a nod or a small wave. After the first day I was brave enough to go into a grocery store and buy some supplies. I'd boasted to Gillian that I was now making dinner at home. "Make dinner for us, then," she'd said, so I'd packed the little gadgets that I needed to wield knives and wooden spoons.

I had a shopping bag. I even had the correct change ready. There was no need to say anything to the woman at the cash register. But I felt bold.

"How are you today?" I said, trying hard to make the words understandable for someone who didn't know me.

She looked blank for a second. She was a tired looking woman in her fifties. When she smiled I could see a side tooth missing. "Very well, thanks, dear. And you?" When she'd packed the groceries into my bag and handed it back to me she said, "Have a lovely day, dear."

"You too," said I.

That was it, that was the extent of my impromptu, unnecessary, but successful conversation with a stranger in London.

I felt as if I'd delivered the opening speech in Parliament. I wheeled on down the street and bought flowers for the girls at a stall on the corner.

I could live in London, I thought. I could take care of myself in this huge, packed city. There were thousands of disabled people here, including my activist friends. I wouldn't be almost alone, as I was in Westerford.

I incubated this thought over the weekend. I wasn't ready to talk about it with Gillian and Kamala. I hadn't looked at the big questions like where, how, with whom, with what practical help, with what money.

Gillian and Kamala escorted me around the sights of London. They showed me the great bridges, Trafalgar Square, the brand-new Globe Theatre on the South Bank. "We'll skip Buck'nam Palace," said Kamala. "Unless you need to pay your respects to imperialism and unearned wealth, Alex." Gillian evidently had not told her of my one-sided relationship with Diana. Buckingham Palace I had no interest in, but I surprised myself by not wanting to go to Kensington Palace either. I didn't want to be one of the gawkers staring up at Diana's windows. I knew she wasn't there, anyway. She was somewhere in Africa or Asia.

Outside the Globe Theatre we sat by the riverside walk looking out over the wide Thames. The sky was banked with solid looking clouds. Families and tourists wandered by, skateboarders and rollerbladers—people on wheels for fun. A man dressed like a Shakespearian clown hailed people with lines from the plays and held out his red and yellow hat for cash. Barges and sightseeing boats swam up and down the river followed by foamy wakes. Gillian produced a bar of nut chocolate and handed around generous chunks.

"Alex," said Kamala. "My friend Linda works with a dance company for disabled and non-disabled people. I've seen them and they're brilliant. They have an open rehearsal on Sunday afternoon. Linda said you're welcome to come. You can just watch, you don't have to do anything. Would that appeal to you?"

I had never heard of a dance company for disabled people. At first it sounded ludicrous to me, like the sing-alongs at Three Wells. Then I remembered the disability conference where one night everyone had danced wildly to disco music, wheelchairs, crutches, callipers and all. I thought of my own long-ago dance with Diana.

I said yes. As long as it was all right just to watch.

The studio in a converted warehouse was walking distance from the flat. Kamala came with me. Her friend was a Chinese woman, tiny and graceful, able-bodied. She moved like a dancer.

"Have fun, bhaiya," Kamala said when she left. She'd started calling me her older brother, which I rather liked.

I followed Linda into a high-ceilinged, windowless studio, brightly lit in the center of the room, dim around the margins where I parked myself.

"Join in whenever you want to," she said. "If you want to."

I saw about a dozen people, most of them disabled. Three were in wheelchairs. They all seemed completely at ease, saying hello, joking, some of them stretching their arms and legs in preparation for the rehearsal. Two were apparently mute, communicating with the others through smiles and energetic gestures. The group was called Wings. Sometimes, Linda said, they developed dances to perform for family members and friends. Today they were going to improvise and explore ideas that might lead to a new piece.

Music rose into the room, unlike any music I'd heard before. High voices sang in a language I didn't recognize, with drums and an electronic instrument holding a long, low note. Linda and the others stopped talking and moved into a wide circle. Arms reached out, heads rolled from side to side, hands waved and fluttered. A bald man circled his wheelchair slowly. My body caught the rhythm. I danced a little by myself in my chair, in the shadows.

There must have been some kind of signal, which I missed. The dancers moved to opposite sides of the room. Two at a time, one from each side, they moved into the empty space in the middle and danced together.

A red-haired girl in a wheelchair rolled out and undulated her arms and torso with the music. Her partner took hold of the wheelchair's arms and pulled it towards him, moving backwards along an invisible serpentine path, their eyes locked on each other. It was like me and Diana. I felt the swoop and spin, the speed of air on skin, our laughing together, the bliss of the dance.

CHAPTER TWENTY

August 30, 1997, late evening

The skeleton dream returns to her in flashes during the day, quickly obscured. It comes back to her again when they sit down, finally, in the hotel restaurant: soft sea air rushing around her, bony arms bearing her home at last. The long, strange day has eroded her and she cannot suppress tears, though whether they are tears of longing, sadness, or exhaustion she cannot tell. In the candle-lit corner of the dining room she sits bowed over the stark white tablecloth. The other diners are staring. Of course they are staring. They would have been staring whether she was crying or not. When have there not been eyes staring at her? She's had more eyes on her than any other human being in the history of the world. Each eye steals something from her, invades her. And yet she has wanted them to look. She has made them look. Now all she wants is to be invisible.

The maître d' hovers in her peripheral vision, evidently concerned, though no doubt more for his restaurant and his other customers than for her. If he is worried on her account it will be only on the shallowest level. How could it be anything else?

He doesn't know her. He knows only what everyone knows, the hysterical princess of the tabloids.

Across the table her lover is murmuring, scolding, trying to take her hands. She can't bear to look at him, at his bovine eyes. She can imagine exactly what they convey, watching her dissolve in this public and inappropriate way—concern, yes, but also embarrassment. Perhaps exasperation, finally.

She hears her lover ordering food for both of them, as though he knows what she would like. He knows nothing, he understands nothing about me, she thinks. He can't imagine how a person could be more complex than he is, which is about as complex as the omelette aux fines herbes he is now choosing for her from the menu. For himself he chooses meat, of course. Steak, rare. It disgusts her to imagine his large white teeth tearing into the piece of flesh, sucking its juices; how his fingers with their tufts of dark hair will lift the napkin to dab at his mouth and cover small belches of satisfaction. The eager sipping of champagne, his glass replenished by the hovering dark-suited presences, while she drips tears onto her untouched food.

She stands up, startling him. "I'm going upstairs," she says before the meal arrives. "Eat if you want. I'm going to sleep." She sees his disappointment. He's hungry. But he's too gallant to let her go alone. "Bring the food to my suite," he calls over his shoulder as he follows her out.

She drops into the chair by the draped window overlooking the boulevard. Paris pulses far below, cars streaming soundlessly in both directions despite the lateness of the hour. It is almost midnight and still raining. He stands behind her, hands on her shoulders, trying to soothe her. "You're tired, my darling. You'll feel better when you eat." She ignores him. He has no idea. Food does not comfort or sustain her, as it does him. Her head is aching. Her eyes feel like burning coals. How can tears make one's eyes burn? She stares and stares out the window, hardly blinking. She feels shrunken, frozen inside her body. Someone knocks on the door and wheels in a trolley with their meal. He urges her again to eat, and then, shrugging, sits down and enjoys it by himself. Bile rises into her throat at the smell of the food. She holds her sleeve against her nose so that she smells linen and her own scent instead. She hears the sounds of him eating, the knife against the plate, the scraping of food onto his fork, the rhythmic masticating and swallowing. She thinks she might scream.

Perhaps he's right, I'm just exhausted, she thinks. Or perhaps I've simply come to the end of my stamina for this crazy dance. Well, it's going to change. Starting tomorrow. She has made so many mistakes, disappointed so many people, in spite of herself. She remembers her own words only two years ago—"I'd like to be a queen of people's hearts"—and she almost sinks to the floor with the embarrassing idiocy of that pronouncement. She wants to embrace the woman who said such a naive and heartfelt thing, to comfort and reassure her. And slap her, for undermining every constructive step with further foolishness. But it is not too late. It can't be too late.

She notices for the first time that the phone by the bed is flashing red. A message.

Her lover is pouring himself another glass of champagne, having eaten her meal as well as his. He reaches for the dessert tray and considers the choices.

She crosses over to the phone and listens.

"Tried you several times," says Hugh's voice. He does not say his name or hers. "Where on earth are you? I thought you'd like to know immediately—PM says yes, he's very interested.

Thinks it could be brilliant though not sure about the land-mine focus. Is public opinion ready blah blah. In other words his own cold feet. I think we can talk him round. But he loves the idea of a full-blown official role. Ambassador-at-large, or somesuch. Wants a meeting in a week or two. Very ticklish for him with regard to you know who. So, absolutely hush-hush at this point. OK? Ring me as soon as you're home."

She puts down the receiver and sits on the edge of the bed, slightly dizzy. The walls recede, a world with different contours appears. She sees herself publicly welcomed back, acknowl-edged and respected. She sees herself carrying on her work with official power behind her instead of against her. She will insist on the landmine focus. She and the PM will have to trust each other.

Her ex and his family will be livid. Spitting tacks. She tries not to gloat. It hasn't happened yet, she reminds herself sternly. But it could. Yes it could!

Her exhaustion has vanished. She wishes she could fly home this instant. She must move, go somewhere, get out of this room. Immediately. Anywhere.

"Darling—let's go back to your apartment!"

He looks at her, surprised. He smiles to see her suddenly ani-mated and happy after her earlier despair. He spoons another mouthful of crème brulée. "I thought you wanted to sleep…" But he understands that she is propelled by forces he doesn't see. He must give her what she wants. "My love," he says. "Of course."

He phones down to the bodyguards, who tell him that the driver has gone home, thinking that they were settled for the night. It's already Sunday. The hotel's security chief will drive them instead.

CHAPTER TWENTY-ONE

Alex

I was awakened by the phone ringing and opened one eye to peer at the clock. A quarter to seven on Sunday morning. I pushed myself up in bed, wondering frantically where Gillian was, trying to remember if she'd got back from Germany yet or not. There couldn't have been a plane crash so early in the morning. Could there? The ringing stopped.

"Oh my god," I heard my mother say in the hallway. My skin went cold. "Unbelievable. How terrible. No, I'll tell him. We'll ring you later. Thanks, Gillian, thanks, dear." Gillian was alive.

What on earth had happened?

My mother appeared in her nightgown and bare feet. "Alex. That was Gillian. There's been a car accident—Diana, in Paris. We should turn on the television."

Bewildered, I levered myself into my chair and into the living room. My mother had the tv on already. The announcer was saying things that didn't make any sense at all. He was saying that Diana was dead. The man's face was stunned and sad. He was saying that there had been a car accident soon after midnight and she was pronounced dead at a Paris hospital at four in the morning. They had tried for hours to resuscitate her.

My mother and I sat grasping each other's hands. It was not possible. It could not have happened. There was a mistake.

Photos and video footage of Diana appeared on the screen, some from Saturday, just a few hours ago, Diana getting into a car, Diana going into a fancy hotel. She was alive last night, so how could she be dead now?

My mother went into the kitchen to make tea. I stared at the screen. It did not make sense to me. Diana dead? No!

"...chased into a tunnel under the Seine by photographers," the man was saying. "Her companion and the driver killed instantly"... "The Prince of Wales is returning from Balmoral and will fly to Paris later this morning..."

I could only take in bits of it. My mother came in with the teapot and cups and sat down again beside me. "Poor girl," she said. "Poor girl." She was close to tears, which surprised me a bit. She'd never been taken with Diana, as far as I knew. I was not crying. There was a kind of membrane between me and the vast grief that had swallowed me. I still could not comprehend what the faces on the screen were saying. There were now three of them, shaking their heads, speaking somberly, offering new information—Diana and her boyfriend were on their way to his apartment, she was wearing a black jacket and white pants, they had flown to Paris from Sardinia in the afternoon. Useless details. All I wanted to know was that it was a mistake, they'd got it wrong, she wasn't dead at all.

I watched for two hours without moving. My tea grew cold. My mother brought me some toast and marmalade but I couldn't eat it.

The cameras shifted to people already gathering on the streets in London. We had all gone to sleep in one world and woken up in another. I saw my own feelings reflected on their faces, the shocked disbelief and dreadful sorrow. Some were furious at the photographers. "They hounded her to death!" said one man said angrily to the television reporter. "We knew they would, in the end!" I hadn't thought about that yet, whether someone was to blame. It was hard enough just to take in the tragedy.

"Alex—I'm so, so sorry. So's Kamala," said Gillian when she phoned again. "I can't believe this has happened. Are you OK?" It sounded as though she was crying. "Her sons, oh god..."

Slowly the reality pierced my mind. Diana was gone. I was left behind in a world that no longer contained her. And it was dawning on me that there were millions like me and Gillian, even billions, engulfed by a personal grief for someone we did not actually know. The television showed distraught and weeping people in the United States, in Denmark and Spain, in New Zealand, in Singapore and Kenya and Russia. Everywhere. Even my cynical father was moved. He and Jess phoned to comfort me with not a hint of sarcasm.

I watched as the prince and Diana's sisters escorted her coffin to the royal plane. I did not let myself imagine her cold body inside that box. She would have come home today, the reporters said. She was looking forward to seeing her children after a month apart. Now she would never see them again. They would never see her.

Church bells rang all day. In the early evening my mother and I went down to the square. It was packed with people, silent except for muffled crying. Bunches of flowers were piled by the Albert clock where Gillian and I had seen her all those years ago.

I'd never before had the experience of knowing that every person in sight felt as I did. No one needed to speak. For once my wheelchair did not set me apart at all.

But it changed, for me, after a few days. I still felt stunned and grief-stricken. I ached for her life so violently cut off, and for her children. But I lost my feeling of kinship with the mourners who poured into the center of London with their unrestrained weeping, their mounds of wilting flowers, their teddy bears and sentimental messages as though Diana could read them. I didn't feel part of that. I couldn't really understand what was going on. It began to seem a bit nuts to me, a bit hysterical, as though there'd been a collective decision to ditch British moderation and make up for hundreds of years of stiff upper lips with a mad mudbath of emotion. I was more sympathetic with the rage that exploded alongside the grief, directed mostly at the photographers who had chased her to her death. I hated them too. Long before this final accident they had taunted and tormented her without mercy. They had deliberately humiliated her in order to profit by her distress. They were like rough children who had finally destroyed their own favorite toy.

There was a growing clamor against the Royal Family for their harsh treatment of Diana, for her husband's betrayal, and their refusal now to join in the weep-fest. Some began to speculate about a conspiracy to kill her, among them her boyfriend's inconsolable father. To me it all seemed part of the prevailing lunacy.

Gillian and Kamala offered to fetch me if I wanted to come to London for the funeral. They didn't mean the funeral itself, which would not include the likes of us, but to be with the crowds in the streets as the cortege passed by. But it didn't attract me at all. I knew that all those people were just like me in their sadness and loss. But I did not want to be part of a massive catharsis.

My mother and I watched Diana's funeral on television. It was a strange fusion of solemn pageantry and the soppiest sentimentality. Her sons walked behind her coffin, alone, no friendly arm around their shoulders, no reassuring glances from their father or grandfather or uncle. Their broken young hearts exposed for all to see. Diana would have been appalled.

I still struggled with believing she was dead. The coffin did not convince me, nor the swampy music, or her brother's furious, anguished outcry in Westminster Abbey.

CHAPTER TWENTY-TWO

August 31, 1997, fifteen minutes after midnight

The security chief from the hotel is drunk. His breath stinks of Ricard. She does not care. She is determined to leave. He leads them to the back entrance and the waiting car, but not before they have been observed by the pack of photographers who have lurked outside the hotel all evening. They jump up, attracting the attention of hotel guests and passersby. In a moment there is a crowd, craning to see. Someone holds an umbrella over her. She suspects that by now she looks a mess, after the long, strained day. She hasn't paused to refresh her make-up or change her crumpled jacket. She gets into the car without a glance at the watchers. The door slams. The Mercedes shoots into the road. Her euphoria about Hugh's message evaporates with the lurch of the car and the squeal of tires. She is suddenly afraid. We should have stayed in the hotel, she thinks, too late. The photographers' cars and motorbikes give chase. She twists in her lover's arms to look out the rain-smeared window. They are close enough to see her face and one of them, emboldened, accelerates his motorbike right up beside her, his bearded grin at the window distorted by streaks of rain like a face in a horror film. "Get away from them!" she screams to the man who is driving. He speeds up. He is cursing to himself in slurred French. The bodyguard is hunched in the front seat, sulking at being roused from his rest. Rain beats hard on the windshield, barely cleared by the wipers. The car is flying at breakneck speed through the wet midnight streets. Too fast, she thinks. Dangerous. I have made another mistake. We're going to crash. It will be my fault. Terror obliterates her thoughts. Her lover's arm is tight around her. She clings to it and glances up at his face. He is looking straight ahead, his mouth clenched. His other hand grips the handle above the door. The car careens around corners and through red lights with the pack on its heels. "Putain!" shouts her lover. "Tu vas trop vite!" The driver ignores him. Close to the river they swerve into the tunnel under the Pont de l'Alma, the bridge of the soul. Metal hurls full force against immovable stone.

Death takes her lover and the driver instantly. It savages the bodyguard but lets him go. The pursuers zoom away to safety except for two who snap the shattered, smoking car and its silent occupants.

She hovers above her crushed body in the ambulance, watching her own untouched, suffering face, the controlled urgency of the doctor and technicians—"We must get her to the operating room immediately." "And if we go too fast she dies."

This is not how it ends, she thinks, puzzled. Not now. I'm going home tomorrow. Today. I have to see my children. Something important is happening next week.

The heart monitor shrills a warning. The ambulance, crawling slowly to spare the precious broken body, stops again. They bend over her with desperate care. A blade hangs a millimeter over the thread that connects her to her life. And falls.

CHAPTER TWENTY-THREE

Alex

I went back to my usual things, writing for the newsletter where I now had a monthly column, traveling to schools all around Devon and Somerset. Devising low-calorie dinners for my mother, who'd started fretting about her weight. I'd thought about Diana almost every day since I was fifteen years old. Those thoughts, or even a momentary image, shot a little spring of delight into my day no matter what else was happening. What would it be like to live without that infusion? I was afraid my life might become colorless and flat.

But I realized, slowly and with surprise, that my life was unchanged. It still made me sad to think of her death, of course. But we didn't know each other, Diana and I. It wasn't like losing Michele. I wasn't Diana's friend or lover, I wasn't her brother or her child. I hadn't lost her, because I had never had her. She was more than anything an idea in my mind. And I could keep that idea forever, if I wanted.

Months after the accident Diana-madness was still in full flood, with weeping and wailing, recriminations and accusations, conspiracy theories, television specials, adulatory websites, over-the-top magazine features. It seemed as though anyone who ever knew her or worked for her had stories to tell. A number of parasites lost no time in selling tabloid interviews and hastily ghostwritten books claiming intimate or torrid relationships with Diana. I tried to prepare myself for some story about her and Adam to come to light, but it didn't. I had no idea where he was or what he was doing, if he was still in the army or not. He didn't seem to matter any more.

I was not prepared for a phone call that came one day while I was working at home. I often ignored the phone, letting the answer machine take a message rather than waiting for a stranger to understand me. But this time I happened to pick it up.

"Alex!" a man said, as though we were old friends. The voice was hearty and unfamiliar. For a wild moment I thought it might be Adam, since I'd just been thinking about him.

"This is Alex Carr." I waited.

"Dave Decker here," he said. "From the Daily Star. I'll get right to the point," he went on. "I'm sure you're a busy man. We've heard that you have a very interesting story to tell. From your schooldays."

I assumed he was talking about Michele, and Adam, though why ever would they be interested all these years later? The Daily Star was the last place I'd want Michele's story to be told. But could I refuse, if it would help other victimized kids?

But the man was continuing. "We heard—and of course I can't tell you how we heard—that you actually danced with our dear departed Diana when you were a teenager. In a wheelchair. Quite a story, eh?"

It shocked me. He was speaking of something that had been

my sole knowledge—except for hers—for twenty-two years. My secret. It was like having a stranger's fingers reach inside me and poke my heart.

"How on earth did you know that?" I said and kicked myself for conceding that what he'd heard was true.

"So what was it like, son? Tell me everything you remember. What did she look like, what was she wearing, did you hold hands, did she flirt with you? Did you fall in love with her? Did it drive you nuts that you were crippled and you couldn't cop a feel? Go ahead, I've got my tape-recorder fired up. Do us a favor, talk slowly, you're not easy to understand, you know. We'll send a photographer around later."

I said nothing.

"Don't be shy, Alex. Go ahead, tell me the story. I bet it was the high point of your life, right? Been thinking about it ever since? How did you feel about her marrying Charles? What about all the boyfriends, eh?"

I found my voice. "Look—Mr. Decker—I don't know how you heard about this but I don't want to talk to you. I have nothing to say. Good bye."

"Wait!" he yelled. "Wait! I didn't tell you the most important part. We can offer you a very nice little package indeed if you'll give us an exclusive on this story. Have yourself a luxury holiday. Get your mother a new car." How did he know about my mother's aging car?

"I'm not interested—"

He cut me off again. "Now don't make any hasty decisions, son. Think about it for an hour or two if you want but let me warn you, we're going to write this story whether we talk to you or not. And we'll write it our way, if you won't work with us here."

I hadn't heard this tone of voice since I was fourteen.

"Come on, now." His manner was wheedling again. "Come on, Alex. You had an experience that every red-blooded man in Britain would die for. Every punter's wet dream. Dancing with Diana when she was just a girl. Virginal but a knockout, right? You must have been a looker yourself, for her to single you out. Even though you were crippled. People want to know about these things, Alex." I heard him puff on his cigarette. "Between you and me, the story's been out there for years but we always assumed the boy was a retard. Then we learned that it was someone who went to university, does a bit of writing himself. And a nice-looking chap, so I hear."

I heard the echo of Adam flattering me in order to humiliate me.

"Leave me alone. Don't ring me again."

I put the receiver down, then took it off the hook. The Daily Star must be scraping the bottom of the barrel for anything new about Diana. Readers wouldn't care about my tame and long-ago story. It sickened me to imagine what Dave Decker would do to juice it up, what he might invent about crippled people, and teenage girls who have the hots for disabled boys. He would never get it right, never in a million years.

It took me a while to calm down. I decided I had to tell my mother when she came home. It meant telling her about Diana and our dance, finally.

My mother looked at me with a small smile. "All these years, Alex, and you kept it to yourself? No wonder she was so important to you."

I shrugged. It seemed all right, now, to let her know.

"Anyway, good for you, sending him away with a flea in his ear."

We tried to figure out how Mr. Dave Decker had heard about it.

"Well, there were lots of people there, girls and boys and teachers, weren't there?" my mother said sensibly. "Any of them could have remembered, once Diana became famous. Maybe one of them talked to a reporter, or became a reporter, or married a reporter. We'll never know."

In twenty years of obsessing about that five-minute dance, I'd never thought about all the other people who were there. I'd deluded myself that it was a moment between me and Diana alone.

But my precious secret was not a secret after all, and never had been.

I almost had to laugh.

Diana had apparently spent most of her last month cruising around the Mediterranean on a yacht belonging to her new billionaire boyfriend and his family. And yet in the middle of it she'd flown to Bosnia to visit landmine victims. I saw a photo that made me ache: Diana, her back to the camera, stands close to a middle-aged woman in a graveyard. Her hands tenderly hold the woman's face. The woman clasps Diana's shoulders. Both are focused only on the other.

And then she went back to the yacht, the boyfriend, the nightclubs and parties with movie stars. She was like two completely distinct people. I couldn't reconcile them. I told myself that the frivolous, luxury-loving Diana was not the real her. But I didn't know, really. Who could say what she herself understood or wanted about her different lives, her different selves? Not me.

There was a rumor that the Labour government was on the

point of offering her an official title, an unprecedented position that would have given her an entirely new kind of power and visibility. But it was most likely just a rumor. The Royal Family would never have sanctioned it.

It had been two years since my visit to London. In my mind, the dream of living there was slowly turning into something that could actually happen. I knew Gillian and Kamala would encourage me. They'd help persuade our parents that it wasn't insane. I paid close attention to anything I heard about disabled people living in London, through the activists' network, or from friends, or, very occasionally, in the news, like when a group of them organized a protest to demand better access to the Underground. People like me lived there, got around, found support. Some had jobs. Some even had families.

I thought about the Wings group that Kamala had taken me to visit. The man and woman who danced together like me and Diana. Afterwards I had wheeled myself back to Gillian and Kamala's flat, my skull ringing with the music, my cells charged with an unfamiliar energy. Away from the wide shopping street the bustle and noise ebbed quickly. The road crossed a small river. In a car you'd hardly notice it was there. I paused beside the black iron railings. I'd been missing my own river with its grand sweeping in and out of the tide, the rhythm of my days since I could remember. This one flowed along toward the Thames like a secret, the water surprisingly fast and clear, long feathery weeds prancing in the current.

ACKNOWLEDGEMENTS

I'm grateful to a number of people in the US and England who helped me learn about the experience of cerebral palsy and disability: Linda Chan, Simon Ford, Wendy Houston, Jennie Kristel, Penny Lacey, Jody Satriani, and Nigel Smith.

I also thank Carolyn and Jim Isaac, Jan Zlotnik Schmidt, Veronica Needa, Felicity Laurence, Richard Wistreich, Jonathan Fox, and my daughter Maddy Fox for reading the manuscript on the subway and missing her very important stop.

Dancing With Diana was inspired by an actual encounter between the teenage Diana and a disabled hospital patient, described in *The Diana Chronicles* by Tina Brown.

ABOUT THE AUTHOR

Jo Salas grew up in New Zealand and now lives in upstate New York. Her short fiction has been published in literary journals and anthologies. Her story "After," in the anthology *Facing the Change: Personal Encounters with Global Warming* was nominated for the Pushcart Prize, and other short stories have won or been shortlisted for awards. Jo Salas's nonfiction publications include *Improvising Real Life: Personal Story in Playback Theatre*, now in a 20th anniversary edition and published in seven translations. *Dancing With Diana* is her first novel.